EX LIBRIS

VINTAGE **CLASSICS**

ROSEMARY TONKS

Rosemary Tonks (1928–2014) was a colourful figure in the London literary scene during the 1960s. She published two poetry collections, *Notes on Cafés and Bedrooms* and *Iliad of Broken Sentences*, and six novels, from *Opium Fogs* to *The Halt During the Chase*. Tonks wrote for the *Observer*, *The Times*, *New York Review of Books*, *Listener*, *New Statesman* and *Encounter*, and presented poetry programmes for the BBC.

ALSO BY ROSEMARY TONKS

ROSEMARY TONKS

Businessmen as Lovers

VINTAGE CLASSICS

1 3 5 7 9 10 8 6 4 2

Vintage Classics is part of the Penguin Random House group of companies
whose addresses can be found at global.penguinrandomhouse.com

Copyright © Rosemary Tonks 1969

Rosemary Tonks has asserted her right to be identified as the author of this
Work in accordance with the Copyright, Designs and Patents Act 1988

First published in Great Britain by The Bodley Head in 1969
This paperback first published in Vintage Classics in 2024

penguin.co.uk/vintage-classics

A CIP catalogue record for this book is available from the British Library

ISBN 9781784879327

Typeset in 10.57/15pt Stempel Garamond LT Std
by Jouve (UK), Milton Keynes
Printed and bound in Great Britain by Clays Ltd, Elcograf S.p.A.

The authorised representative in the EEA is Penguin Random House Ireland,
Morrison Chambers, 32 Nassau Street, Dublin D02 YH68

Penguin Random House is committed to a sustainable future
for our business, our readers and our planet. This book is made
from Forest Stewardship Council® certified paper.

1

There's a bit of a train that shunts around Paris from the Gare du Nord to the Gare de Lyons. If you've just crossed the Channel and you're going straight on to Italy, you have to sit in it while it does this. Nearly everyone gets off at the Gare du Nord. The thing is to walk down the carriage and see what sort of human odds and ends are left over. Even really glossy people tend to look forlorn; the only travellers with staying power are jolly young women travelling together. Married couples are hopeless. Single men just have to get off (they know they ought to be flying anyway). But if you can stand the boredom (and it's all part of the big obstacle race to get down to Italy) after the feeling that you may disintegrate, that you've forgotten where you're going, and don't care anyway, up comes a mood of sickly good cheer. It's like the old wartime cheerfulness, if anyone can remember it.

They take the tablecloths away, and you sit on at a table of dark green rexine leather. There's a lamp giving out a feeble glimmer, with a fluted shade of plastic parchment, and a solid brass base with a switch in it. You switch it on and off. That intensifies the boredom.

Don't imagine from all this that I'm alone. I am not. I've got Caroline with me, and we talk the whole time.

'Italy, Carol! Aunt Evie's house! Island life!'

'I know. I can't believe it. We'll wake up in Tuscany tomorrow morning, all green and sunny. Have you noticed how the train seems to slide along in quite a different restful, contented way directly we get into Italy?'

'Of course. It *purrs*. I say, we'll have one of those non-breakfasts: bang, bang, "*Buon giorno, signorina. Caffè?*"'

'And before you can say "Jack Robinson" he's into the sleeping compartment and counting the bosoms. Then he gives you a paper thimble with boiling black ink in it.'

'And chats you up. Actually, when I came down two years ago I scuttled mine by being dressed *first.* You should have seen his face: no bosoms!'

'So what did he do?'

'He came in and jammed his manhood against my knee and slowly, slowly poured the coffee. I think it was a better deal than bosoms.'

'Honestly! Still, they are awfully jolly, and all a bit nervous, just like women.'

'Mustn't have a draught on their heads, otherwise they go berserk. I wonder why?'

'The French are just the same. It's murder. As soon as you cross the Channel people go around holding their heads. Big strong men too.'

'They're the worst of the lot. Why don't they wear balaclava helmets and have done with it?'

'Hum. I think I know why.'

We enter a tunnel, and at once the lights go down.

'Mean pigs. Have you got your travelling torch?'

Caroline hates the dark, and so do I. We're veteran travellers, after years of brute suffering. I've got a torch, matches, an inflatable rubber ring (for floods), glucose tablets, migraine tablets etc. etc.

This train is so mean with its light I can only just see her across the table. She's my second cousin, very goodlooking and neurotic. At the moment, I like her company better than anyone else's I can think of. She's got a little chuckle that comes on when she describes some awful thing that has happened in life (i.e. every day); sometimes it's a greedy little chuckle, and sometimes it's sexy. It tells me to be a materialist, and I love it. It means safety, warm houses, new clothes, and friends to stay with all over the world.

More tunnels. And in between, the cardboard crusts of buildings seen from the back; they're all very tall and often finished at the side in a point, like a new india-rubber before you've started rubbing out with it. Thank God we don't have to pretend we're interested; we've both passed the stage when we could bear to travel with a woman who calls out: 'There's a lovely old church!' or leans forward and says with a nasty smile: 'Why don't you fly?' I certainly like being older and getting away from all that dish-wash, and I say to Caroline:

'You know, Carol, I really like ageing. It's excellent. I don't care if I do slow down.'

'I don't think people do slow down at all. It's a complete lie. They go faster and faster. Look at Killi. When I first married him he was *languid*. Now he's over-revved all the time from making money and counting it.'

'Killi has masses of charm.'

'Killi has been *impossible* for the last four years. He gets above himself, like all men who make a lot of money. I really had to smack him last Saturday evening.'

'Gosh.'

'I said: "You've been so horrid I'd simply like to give you a sharp slap somewhere. Where would you like it?"'

'What *did* he say to that?'

'He said he was tender all over – and his great big freckled forearms were sticking out of his pyjama jacket like a prize-fighter's. So I said: "Luckily for you I'm not a dog or I'd simply go ahead and bite you".'

'That's probably what he wants.'

'No fear. Killi only has sex for balance-sheets these days.'

'What do you have sex for, Carol?'

'Oh, I don't know. A linen cupboard full of linen, I suppose. You're the only one I know who has sex for sex.'

I turn my head away, because I'm going to say something serious, and say quite quietly:

'I only have sex for Beetle, you know.'

Beetle is my great love. He's just forty; he has a beautiful round chin, and where the pale skin of his face gets dark there, you can be sure of picking up the smell of old-fashioned shaving creams. There are other old-fashioned things about him: he's good-tempered and reliable, he gives me moral support, and he balances my emotional books without having to give the truth a twist to do it (I'd jump on that straight away). He looks his best in a dark blue Boulevard St Michel suit, like a pallid, elegant, six-foot head boy who knows everything, has superb manners and a perfect sense of history, but without having lived long enough in the world to have become either bitter or disillusioned. He works for Reuters, or Reuters works for him, in a glass office filled with shiny machines. He was brought up in the country and knows the price of things, people, and himself, without being afraid of it or making others afraid – something that in Killi would be inspired and extrasensory. Beetle's great art is the ability to handle life and play with it. Out of the play comes his income and our jokes and evenings of husky laughter. It was Beetle who gave me this old Italian phrase book I'm shining my torch on. He got it in a back street in Naples, and he says it's the most valuable object he possesses. 'Manual of Conversation, With Italian figured pronunciation, for english tourist in Italy, by Prof. Carlo Barone. First part: Wowels'.

Caroline can see this upside down, and begins to laugh.

'Look up railway journeys and romance.'

'OK. Here's "Familiar Conversation" . . . hum, what's this: "Going to Bed." "John, give me a boot-jack, my slippers, and my night-cap." "There they are, sir." "Have you closed the shutters?" "Yes, sir, but perhaps you had better leave them open." "Why so?" "To see the sun the sooner." "I declare myself unworthy to see the orb of day." "At what o'clock must I waken you, sir? At six o'clock?" "John, I will discharge you, if you are unlucky enough to waken me before ten –"'

'Ha! Sounds like you all right. Discharging people and sleeping late.'

' "Draw the curtains of my bed. O blissful bed! Blessed be the man who invented beds!" '

'I don't believe it.'

' "*O, beato letto! Benedetto chi ha inventato i letti!*" '

'I can guess what comes next.'

'It doesn't. He just goes to sleep. And he's not even queer. Listen to this: "My dear Friend, you bore me considerably; let me sleep. Good night".'

'Nothing like coming to the point.'

'I can't find railway journeys. Hang on ... "Will you have the kindness to tell me where is a box of letters?"'

'That's really familiar conversation.'

'Would you like: "At a Coffee-house"?'

'Not unless there's a part for me.'

I must admit I've been reading out these quotes rather well, with the throttle on for the male voices. And Caroline is getting broody. She suddenly bends over the book, and puts on a greedy, elderly voice:

'"Waiter, pour me out a *good lot* of coffee!"' Snuffle, snuffle.

She spoils it by laughing at her own voice. But I pick it up reasonably politely.

'"Physicians declare it to be a beverage very injurious to the health".'

'"Yes,"' (Caroline is far too nasal) '"they pretend that it is a slow poison, and they are right".'

'"Do you think so?"' (It's funny the way directly we take parts, Caroline has all the long, meaty paragraphs, while I seem to be whittled down to a sort of interviewer.)

'"Only look at that old gentleman reading the newspaper yonder!"'

There's a convulsive movement from some seat far away in the dim carriage.

This time I've got quite a good line, and give it strongly:

'"What, him with the perfectly white hair?"'

' "The very same," ' says Caroline with extreme satisfaction. ' "How old do you think he is?" '

Someone has put down a pair of glasses on the dark green rexine tablecloth and is making turning-round movements. I say casually:

' "He may have seen four score years." '

' "Well then," ' (Caroline has a thick chunk ahead and is really warming to it) ' "that old man has frequented this coffee-house for the last forty years, coming here regularly for his poison every day that Heaven grants him". '

Yes, whoever it is *is* staring at us, and we'll have to shut up. I murmur, hardly above a whisper:

' "Coffee must be a very slow poison indeed. But weak tea deranges my stomach; strong tea suits my palate, but it is too exciting and prevents me from sleeping." '

' "It is a beverage which none but ladies can properly appreciate," ' Caroline finishes complacently.

There's a jolt, and we are out into the daylight again. This time it's the real thing. A long grey platform and into the Gare de Lyons. Big, shadowy cavern. Hullo: what a lot of people! I've never seen quite so many all on one platform.

'I say, Carol, they look rather fierce.'

'They do, don't they? It's just the French look these days, since de Gaulle.'

We've both dressed ourselves up like women of the world in order to get porters. Caroline has all her rings on. (She takes them off to go through the English customs. If they see a ring or two which isn't to do with marriage they open *everything*. Also, she takes care not to laugh or look happy. This has exactly the same effect. The sex war is so different in each country. The main thing is to swot it all up conscientiously in advance. For example, today we've got on skirts down to our knees, especially for Paris.)

On the platform we soon get lost inside this extraordinary crowd. They're commuters, and have a grey, fretful air. Our luggage makes an island, and we stick to it. An elderly Englishwoman seems to be with us on the island. A megaphoned voice urges the crowd to hurry, and some of the faces are getting frenzied. There's the danger of being trampled. What elbows!

The Englishwoman turns to me suddenly and says in an intimate tone:

'You haven't by any chance a thermometer, have you?'

'A *thermometer*? Not . . . at this very moment.'

(The French are flowing past at the rate of six a second.)

'Oh. Well. Never mind.' She draws in a breath and holds it. 'You see, I think I've got a cold coming on. And if I *have,* I shall have to turn round and go straight home again. Because it'll *ruin* my holiday.'

And don't think she isn't serious. I'm fighting for my beachhead, but I've got time to remember that five minutes ago we were actually stupid enough to laugh at an old Italian phrase book and to read out sections of it to one another. What idiots! As though life wasn't already ahead of us. Oh; I'm going to do something rather nasty now. I can feel it coming on. Am I going to resist it? No, I don't think I am.

'Wowels!' I call out sharply to Caroline.

She turns her head.

'*Dov' è il termometro?*'

'*Nel giardino, idiota,*' she answers shortly. And gripping

a big blue porter who has suddenly appeared: '*Porteur, qu'est-ce qui se passe?*'

'*Ils font la grève, ma petite dame.*'

'*La grève? Mais nous devons prendre l'express pour Rome! Est-ce que vous croyez qu'on pourra l'attraper?*'

'*Je ne sais pas. Peut-être. Personne ne sait.*'

'*Alors, nous pouvons demander sur le quai. Voulez-vouz nous aider? Nous avons ces quatres valises – pardon, madame – six. Voici les billets pour le wagon-lit.* Boo – just our luck,' to me.

'How on earth we're going to get up the platform, I don't know. I'm nearly running to stay in the same position as it is.'

'It's all right. He'll mow them down with his trolley, like Boadicea. You know how people hate wheels in among their legs.' Caroline is right, but I haven't time to tell her so because the Thermometer is at my ear:

'I had one before once "(a cold)" when I got to Brussels. And I simply felt I couldn't face the Hook.'

'Certainly not.'

'So I'm wondering whether it wouldn't be more sensible to go back now, before it's too late . . .'

'Well, it's very strange, but I, personally, always feel as though I've got a cold coming on when I start travelling.' (We are all three in a bunch behind the porter who is driving his trolley forward steadily.) 'Why don't you hang on until we get to the Rome Express? Then you can ask the Wagon-Lit man for a thermometer. He's bound to have one.'

'Oh do you think so?'

'Positively. It's part of his job.'

'You are a comfort. Perhaps I should try to hold out just a little longer.'

'I should. You can lie down the moment we get on to the train.'

If you tell someone they can lie down, they often get the feeling that they're being kept out of life and may be missing something. The Thermometer perks up no end when I say that. She stops looking brave, and says with a touch of authority:

'I'm feeling much better already, thank you.' She checks up on her gloves and handbag in case someone (myself) should try to take them away from her under the pretext of forcing her to 'lie down'.

'The students,' says Caroline, who has been gabbling with the porter, 'are having a revolution. And also the factory workers of Renault. De Gaulle is out of the country. The porter thinks our train may have been cancelled.'

'Why on earth didn't the travel agents tell us before we started?'

'Because they'd never sell a single ticket if they told the truth. Just look at that!'

They talk about people 'seething', but what one really notices are the hundreds of thousands of white faces without movement or expression on top of the bodies which are 'seething'. The Thermometer couldn't 'lie down' at the moment even if she wanted to; there isn't room.

Quai 22. Hell! It's miles away. This porter is excellent. He's got slow, weary shoulders which he expands when people get near him. Bam. Biff. Our tips are going up minute by minute.

The loudspeakers keep blasting off overhead. I'm rather

enjoying it. We could end up sleeping in a bathroom in the Cité Universitaire. Or the Ritz. Or in a gutter. I remember once falling into a gutter in Soho and finding it surprisingly comfortable; the trick is to get your head well into the hollow and then fold your arms across your stomach, and relax *completely* . . .

Here's the train! A miracle. It's steaming, and there are blocks of ice with rounded, slippery edges and complex white jewellery inside, going into the busy end of the restaurant car. These strikers have a nice sense of priorities after all. Shall I stop and get two pink tickets for first service dinner? Can't. The Thermometer is tottering, she's seen the train and all she really needs now are a pair of collapsible crutches, she's simply wobbling to pieces. What a useful thing a cold is.

'This way. Oh, you're number seventeen. No, it's not over the wheels. And you've got an awfully nice man. He's Italian, so you're bound to be all right. You know how they look after women travelling alone. It's not like England, you know, they really like women over here. He'll fuss over you with his first-aid kit.'

A few minutes later Caroline says:

'You know what's happened, don't you? We've missed the pink tickets for first service.'

'Don't say that!'

Suddenly we're both up against one of the brute facts of life, and stare at one another. Never mind the Revolution. Second service on the Rome Express starts after ten p.m. and takes *hours*, so you don't get any sleep. I don't feel like digesting a mutton chop at eleven o'clock at night. Damn the Thermometer.

'Let's go and shake her.' That's Caroline.

'While we were unselfishly wheedling and coaxing her into her compartment, we were missing our pink tickets.'

'We'll buy a bottle of wine and some rusks' (what pathos) 'and go to bed early.'

'Has it come to this? Rusks and cheap wine!' I keep laughing, but in fact I'm quite depressed. Caroline is good at topping up a situation with words like 'rusks'. What she means is that it's my fault for helping the Thermometer. If *she* had helped her, it would probably have been 'ham rolls'.

We spend an hour waiting for the train to start. We're sharing a sleeper, and when we've hung up our coats and washed our hands, we're at the mercy of rumours just like everyone else. You get to know certain parts of the world far too well at such times. And the people in the other carriages soon drop into their circus rôles. There's a Mafia Italian two doors away, not more than twenty-five years old, a born bully; he's got a great head with whiskers growing around it which is a hundred years out of date. Into one of the cracks in this head he's stuck a khaki cheroot, and keeping the eyes above it half-closed, he stands half in and half out of his compartment. When Caroline and I go along the corridor past him, he swells up his chest so that all the cords on his string vest are tensed under his transparent nylon shirt. I think Caroline quite likes this, but I do see it could be dangerous. On either side of our compartment are wizened-up Italian businessmen, the lizard type. Then there's a sort of Persian in a camel-hair coat, with dark glasses and a lot of white hair. He seems curiously friendly.

At last the train starts. An hour late; but even so

normality is at once reasserted. We glide out of the station leaving the loudspeakers chanting and the great crowd still out of control. But we – out of the crisis by the skin of our teeth – are peaceful, and harmonising ourselves with the movement of the train, we pick up books or begin to think our own thoughts. I think away for about ten minutes; inside my head I'm fully occupied insulting someone who's interrupted a lecture I'm giving (I lecture on English at certain colleges of education and sometimes I get hecklers). After I've insulted him a couple of times, I begin to get warmed up and start the scene all over again: 'Another greengrocer with a Viva Zapata moustache . . .' Caroline has much the same wilful expression on her face. She's taken off her rings and is staring at them; a sure sign of danger in a woman. I guess she's talking to Killi ('It isn't the adultery that bothers me, it's the bad behaviour.')

Without warning, the corners of my mouth tremble and my eyes fill with tears. I've just remembered (as though I could forget it for an instant) my mother's death. This great grief lies inside my head with folded wings; it seems to be asleep for ten minutes or twenty minutes at a time. Then the wings open; certain attitudes of her head appear, sentences full of joy and wisdom are spoken again by her, again she asks me for help (and always so courteously) and in return I am negligent, and she dies. And all over again I feel the gaping hole behind me in my life, that hole which is torn open freshly every day, and where the wind will always blow in unless I can somehow stop it up with good memories. My uneasy conscience makes me say softly:

'Oh, Carol.'

Caroline is so kind. She plays it this way:

'You know, Mimi (using my nickname), if she'd been with us today, she would have made the most awful scene. And we'd be in a complete mess by now. And you and she would have had a row.'

'Yes, I know. I don't mind her dying. It's the tragic sudden way it happened. You see hundreds of obituaries to lumpish businessmen or scientists with lantern jaws, but one of the most delicate, amusing women in Europe dies all alone and nobody writes an obituary to say: "She made life more amusing for about a hundred people."'

'That's because it's such a rotten century. We're all dumb, grey, brutal economists.'

'You're not allowed to mourn over someone. People just get snappy with you. When I dared to mention to X (an old friend) that she'd died, he just looked over my shoulder and said: "Yes, I heard." Couldn't even put together one commiserating sentence.'

'It's fantastic. The only comfort is that no one will give him a thought when he dies. In fact, I've already stopped thinking about him, so he might as well be dead as far as we're concerned.'

The train has come to a halt without our noticing it. Where are we? Tonnerre: a town, but also the heart of the French countryside.

We go to bed, talking around my great grief with curative sentences. I'm grateful, undress neatly, and don't fuss. I'm wearing pyjamas; Caroline, who is better off than I am, has an important nightdress with long sleeves. I realise that if I don't pull out of my grief it will affect my health, and I'll never be able to fascinate Beetle with nightdresses. The trouble is I know perfectly well why my mother died:

nightdresses, but no Beetle. She looked over her life carefully and, not finding enough of the things she considered necessary for a life, she decided to die. And I know very well that I have to go on thinking over and over her life and death until I 'get it right'.

Oh, here's a delicious breath from the dark countryside – it's blown in at the top of the window. We close the window with a great chromium handle like a jemmy; it's stiff and could rupture an old man. Down with the blind: and then we lie in our bunks, murmuring to one another like two good children.

There's continuous argumentation from the corridor: the Italians discuss and re-discuss the situation loudly, walking up and down the train. Impossible to sleep. I've got a bottle of eau-de-cologne, because I'm trying to learn to use it in order to render myself up to life as a fragrant traveller whose flesh is cool at any moment of crisis. In fact I never know quite where to put it or in what quantity. I have an idea that it contains a scouring ingredient, like Ajax, and so the cleft between my head and my ears is obviously the place. Splash. It stings a bit.

Voices outside our door grow louder, and (is it my imagination?) drunker. A French mezzo is making a row with our attendant who was lying full-length along the corridor, having given up his bunk to a woman traveller. I can hear some *'vous n'êtes pas gentil'* nastiness. Our attendant is spot on for such situations though, and replies with exactly the right note of craven whimpering which is in the musical score for pleasing an eighteen-year-old revolutionary. They get through the verbal Chopin polonaise without blows, but Caroline hisses:

'Quick, lock the door. They'll rape us and bag our rings.'

Of course. Why didn't I think of it? Rape and rings. I'm out of bed in one go. Door locked. Very cautiously, we raise the blind a fraction. Caroline says:

'Ha! They've made a fire on the line, and they're standing round it, *drinking*.'

'Crikey. What fun. Do we join in?'

'Suppose they burn the train?'

'We climb out of the window and make a run for that long grass. Then we strike out for the nearest farmhouse. I'm rather looking forward to it.'

'We might have to settle here, and get married and bring up children all over again.'

'If only we had one of those inflatable plastic houses. You just go into a field and blow it up.'

'What we really need are plastic bicycles. We could blow them up and *cycle* into Italy.'

'Italy! Were we ever going to Italy?'

'Wowels.'

'*Buon giorno, signorina.*'

'Swimming slowly in warm clear water.'

2

'But *you got here.*'

'Yes, after two nights on that futile train.'

'Do you remember the white mist swirling around the revolutionaries and their fire the following morning?'

'Do I not! And the Calabrian ambassador having his private plane sent for – he was a very pretty gorilla, aged about twenty-six and dolled up to the eyebrows. Our Wagon-Lit man had to carry his trunk.' I make a trunk-carrying pantomime with the top half of my body.

'And he had his court photographer with a little ciné camera photographing it all. Mimi was shutting our window and he photographed her,' says Caroline.

'I made *enragé* faces so as to make it worth his while.'

'They just stepped off the railway track into the long grass; trunk, ambass., cameraman and all, and the grasses swished to behind them. And the silence literally came and buzzed in your ears after that.'

We get it all out because it's our story, and our hunger and sleeplessness are embedded in it. We want sympathy. Rupert listens. Rupert is Sir Rupert Monkhouse, one of our neighbours in the English colony on Livone. He looks about fifty-nine and is an archaeologist. He's got an absolutely square face, every time you see it it's squarer than it was the time before, and just as you're on the point of saying: 'Quick! A piece of pumice-stone to rub off those corners,' he smiles brilliantly, exactly like a little boy being given jelly. He gets a great deal of sparkling light into his eyes, and from then on you're happy and wait quite patiently until he does it again. In conversation he hates factual inaccuracy or words mispronounced, and is short about it. When you become sloppy you find yourself on his black list. Having tea with him is the best entertainment there is in Europe between four o'clock and six in the afternoon, except kissing Beetle, of course. Still, Beetle will be here soon, so I can have both!

We're having breakfast on the terrace under the fig tree. It's half past ten. In the sunny air, we already look different, almost beautiful. There's a little lemon tree in the centre of the terrace, plus lemons, and there are arum lilies with throats like the funnel in a wrapped-up linen napkin. Red roses grow up the trunk of the fig tree. The rosemary and lavender bushes are so thick, so aromatic, it's like going through the heated cosmetic department in Harrods. Lizards – skinny businessmen just like the ones in the train with their clothes off – warm themselves up in different positions.

All hornets are huge, but the ones in this garden are the size of robins. Their blue-black fibre-glass plates catch every bit of sun and sizzle, and they're too *busy* to stop over the breakfast table for marmalade or anything else. There's a perpetual glamorous *fluttering* over the flowers; all the witchcraft which began a *corps de ballet* is here, with these flouncy butterflies.

Caroline, who is already beginning to turn into a butterfly, says:

'Then they made a collection for the engine-driver in a dirty white paper bag.'

'You were stationary at the time, of course,'

'Of course. So he consented to drive us south, against his will, and in the teeth of the revolution, just out of the kindness of his heart, once he'd got the paper bag *full* of money.'

'All the signals were against us, so it was hell going through the Alps, Rupert. Just think of all the corners.' And as I say it I really feel sorry for us, because the Alps are literally all corners. 'The engine-driver kept getting out and running on ahead to see if there was anything coming.'

'It sounds more Russian than French.'

'It was. Loaves of bread being bartered across the tops of hedges every time we stopped. And the train tooting and whistling to get people on board again. Or sometimes just gliding on without a sound; diabolical. But don't think *we* got any bread.'

'You didn't? I should have thought you two together, working as a team . . .'

'The Wagon-Lit end of the train always stopped outside the stations, and well away from the loaves. They locked the doors between the carriages, so it meant making a run for it. And we never knew how much time there was.' I'm getting long-winded, so Caroline says sharply:

'The couchettes got the loaves.'

'Someone got off at Modane for an orangeade, and we never saw him again.'

'I see. Well, perhaps you were wise. It's a pity to miss Italy for a loaf of bread and an orangeade.'

'That's what we thought. But Rupert, *Rupert*, the dismal aching misery of the miles! Inching along, all pinched with hunger.' I feel so pinched having said this that I instantly butter myself another piece of toast. 'And when we got to Turin!'

'Yes? What? Quickly!'

'We missed the loaves again.'

'No! I can't bear it.' Rupert begins to load up a spare breakfast plate with a decent helping of butter and marmalade.

'There was a terrible crowd, just like the one we'd left behind in Paris.'

Rupert bites his toast, and mumbles:

'The Italian elections, of course. I'd forgotten that. Free passes for the whole family to vote.'

'But this time we were weaker, due to fasting; it saps your nerve, you know.'

'Undoubtedly.'

'When, suddenly, out of the blue, there was our Wagon-Lit man with eight cartons of pre-packed meals, each containing half a chicken, bottle of vino, plastic plates, knives and forks, and plastic restaurant fly!'

'Well, thank heavens for that!' Rupert stops eating and leans back in his garden chair. Butterflies drift over us.

Caroline and I are ruthless, and we give it to him almost together:

'They'd been ordered by the *others*. All the men in our carriage, Rupert. And, Rupert, we, the only two young (or youngish) women travelling together had been *excluded*.'

'I wonder if Restituta could boil me an egg? Four minutes, if possible . . . I may even need some beef tea . . .'

'Then there was a knock on the door of the compartment, and it was the Persian in the camel-hair coat and dark glasses.'

' "Him with the perfectly white hair".'

'Do you know what he gave us?'

'Mimi, be kind –'

'*Four* biscuits.'

Rupert squirms in his chair, looking worn out. He says hopefully:

'You ate them?'

'Never! We rejected them. We said we didn't want to deprive him, and it was perfectly all right. I think I would have choked, wouldn't you, Mimi?'

I've got my mouth full, and nod. And then grasp my throat to show how I would have choked on being given four biscuits by a Persian. It seems to me that Caroline has a very odd expression on her face; almost paralysed. It doesn't seem to be part of the game. Rupert has seen it too, and we both try to squint round and follow the direction she's looking in. Oh! A visitor. Oh! It's . . .

' "Him with the perfectly white hair!" ' says Caroline.

She's shaken to the roots, and so am I. We drop the nonsense-making and take up our normal play-acting. A pity. Caroline will have to be Caroline Vandeveldt, Killi's wife. Rupert instantly puts on his archaeological knighthood, which he does by becoming tense, clever and remote. I'm hideously formal; my brain fills with lecturer's rhubarb. I've got my nasty little smile on (Mona Lisa interviews you for a job).

The Persian comes very slowly up the scented pathway. I suppose we must seem intimidating, frozen around a table like this, like some eternal breakfast party.

Why doesn't he say something? Boo!

Ah, here it comes. All charm, oil, tenderness, and middle-eastern simpatico.

'Is it Mrs Killi Vandeveldt? What a pleasure to meet you, Mrs Vandeveldt. Forgive me for intruding like this, so early in the morning. I wondered if your husband . . . ?'

Damn. He's a friend of Killi's, so Caroline's got to be nice to him. And he's going to pretend he's never seen us before! People are weird. Still, Killi's world is the money world, and once you're through the sound barrier there, they're all as mad as hatters and con one another to death. Caroline's not going to let him get away with it; she's all gentle and puzzled:

'But surely we met on the train?'

Split-second pause after being clean bowled.

'Why, yes. We did. Then it was you, in the carriage? Really, so embarrassing, two ladies alone in such circumstances. It must have been a nightmare for you. I admired you both so much – from a discreet distance of course (tee-hee) – from my solitary berth.'

He's actually going to try to cash in on his loneliness, in the face of that carton of pre-packed chicken and vino! Admiring us from his solitary berth (while eating and drinking)! I've just remembered, they were Peak Frean biscuits with scalloped edges and little needle-holes in them.

'My cousin and I' (you've got to hand it to Caroline!) 'rather enjoyed the French Revolution, and we wish it the greatest possible success. Mr Cohn-Bendit is a friend of my eldest son, James.' Curiously enough, this is more or less true. The children arrived by air yesterday, full of information. (Like Killi, their social life is too jam-packed for long train journeys.) James is fourteen and met Cohn-Bendit a few months ago. The children are down on the beach at the moment, checking their swimming equipment, inflating lilos, and performing other innocent tasks.

'An unforgettable moment in French history. The franc will have to be devalued in October.'

'November.' That's Rupert teasing him.

The Persian brings hoods down over his eyes and shuts off his whole face for a minute as though he's closing the Bourse, so as to appear to accommodate November in his calculations, out of politeness to Rupert. I'm uneasy about this man. He's too polite. He's undoubtedly accustomed to getting his own way, but he's unlikely to get bored with the trivial side of this. That's sinister. If it's necessary to fawn, he'll fawn. He's a financial sock-darner in an age when people throw away socks with holes in them. He's – painstaking. He's pretending, and pretending very well, to use his intelligence at our breakfast table.

Caroline is interested too. I can tell that because she gets up in order to show off her lace wrap – absolutely white lace that would give you a healthy pink skin, even if you were a lizard.

'Ah, your English complexions,' says the Persian, half joking but with some straight admiration. I do see that we need men like this to say this sort of thing.

'You must come and meet the children,' says Caroline graciously; 'they're very good with francs.'

Hullo: she's showing him her intelligence too, by giving

him a side-swipe. I do believe they like one another. We're miles away from the four biscuits. Or is she just doing it for Killi? Caroline's very loyal.

He kisses our hands expertly (half an inch above the hand) and goes off into the sunshine.

'Well!'

'Was he or was he not on the train when it shuffled round Paris, Mimi?'

'He was. Disguised as a little old lady.'

'He thought we were trying to guess his age.'

'He was afraid of being exposed.'

'So he tested us by giving us four biscuits.'

'No. He genuinely wanted to get to know us . . .'

'So he gave four biscuits.'

'Caroline, do stop it! He knew who we were all the time. And he assumed that anyone married to Killi would at least be travelling with a hamper from Fortnums. So he thought he would do something "amusing".'

'Only too late he realised that there was no hamper when we bit the hand that fed us.'

'So he hurried round to make it up before we told Killi.'

Caroline says sombrely:

'He's just a greedy old Persian who's frightened of flying, that's all.'

'Nonsense. He's stuck on you, and he put up with a horrible train journey in order to get to know you.'

'He's stuck on Killi, and he put up with a horrible train journey in order to get to know Killi's wife.'

Rupert says firmly:

'Well, now he knows her. And I want to go on to my own troubles. After all, Mimi, I'm putting up Beetle for you, and David Rety. And that means I've got a house full. And here's another of them writing to me that he wants to come down . . . could you clear your storeroom?'

Rupert wants us to put somebody up. A journalist called Ronald Dyson. I remember him vaguely. TV Middle-East correspondent, Peter Pan view of how to live life and an acid, barking cough like a pistol-shot. I quite liked him. But having him in the house . . . with all his habits . . . Why not Beetle at that rate? His habits are excellent; people would think themselves lucky even to get a view of his habits. He's always rapid and quiet. He puts white stuff on to shave, and makes dark roads in it. He always cuts himself. It's the most satisfying process for both of us. Then he gives me his new chin, it's chilly and healthy like a newly whetted stone and slightly luminous with sex-appeal. He's fond of rubbing his chin on me, as part of love-making . . . Oh, it's a good thing Beetle's fixed up with Rupert! Of course it's Rupert's way of looking after his safety, having journalists to stay. They don't want to marry him (he's a widower) and they might write about him. What he really needs is a rich worldly woman who would say: 'No one wants your dingy little shop-soiled title, so relax. The only thing I'm interested in is your body,' and marry him.

'Serve him right, actually,' says Caroline when Rupert's gone. 'I adore Rupert, but he does need marrying. There's never any food in his house. Starvation Hall, the grape-vine says.'

'And the grape-vine never lies.'

'Never.'

'You notice he made a jolly good breakfast while he was here.'

'Asking for boiled eggs!' Caroline's chuckling noise is *wicked*.

'And it wasn't a joke.' I'm laughing outright. 'I once spent a whole evening with him in Rome and he gave me a toasted sandwich.'

'He likes women to pick at their food.' We're desperately unfair and laugh heartily at everything we say.

'Beetle stayed with him in England for the weekend and took a whole suitcase of food, a cold pheasant, two boxes of dates, a hank of bananas, and he even went into the local butcher's for some ham, and there was a queue, and who do you think was in it?'

'Rupert!'

'Rupert! And he interrogated Beetle on the spot. Beetle says it's the only time he's ever blushed. And do you know, they had gigantic meals, all the weekend. And Rupert insisted upon carrying his case out to the car at the end of it, and said how heavy it was.'

We're thoroughly pleased with ourselves, and much too fond of Rupert to bother to describe his good points. Rupert is quite sexy, you know. Caroline once described him as being 'as sexy as a nun' and that's great praise from Carol. She says you can always tell what time of the year it is in England: 'First appearance of nuns, Americans, and Rupert – it must be spring!' or 'Killi's got his suffering, martyred look on. You can set your thermostat by it. It's winter.'

I go into my bedroom and do some more unpacking. I even start humming. Gosh, I'm happy. It's disgraceful. Surely I should be suffering? Just a second: what's that curious ache along my jaw? I must have had it for some time. Don't say it's toothache! I stand very still, and try to feel how bad it is. Hmm, pretty bad. Ache, ache, ache. I sit down mournfully on the cotton beige bedcover. Just my luck. I've probably got an abcess. There's no doubt about it, I'm harbouring a rotten tooth and Beetle with his strong, perfect, fresh-tasting teeth will reject me out of hand.

The Italian phrasebook is on the bed, and I can't resist diving into it, because I seem to remember Beetle reading out some very funny pieces about toothache, and I've certainly got to prepare myself for an Italian dentist.

I can hear Restituta sweeping out the great chequered stone floor of the lounge with that fluffy nylon broom. Then she'll dust the two cases of butterflies by the big open fireplace. My window's wide open, and now and again it's so quiet I imagine I can even hear Rupert's parting footsteps as he scrunches up the unmade road to his house on the mountainside.

I read:

"I have a hollow tooth that makes me suffer dreadfully."

"Sit down in that armchair, madam, throw your head back and open your mouth wide. Your mouth is pretty clear of teeth!"

"Alas! I have but eight left."

"Then you have lost twenty-four."

"Impossible!"

"It is very certain. In each jaw there are four incisives, two canines, and ten grinders, which makes thirty-two teeth in all."

"Ah! Why did I not consult you sooner?"

"The harm is done; there is no remedy. Let me see the tooth. Is it that one?"

"Yes, sir. Could you not stop it up?"

"Stopping up teeth is only a palliative."

"You will pull it out for me then?"

"No, madam, I will extract it."

"But that is very painful."

"Not at all. It is a very easy operation, even not unaccompanied vith (sic) a certain pleasure . . . when it is over. Come, be courageous."

"But, sir . . ."

"Let me only take out the cotton you have put in the hollow of the tooth. – Crack! There it is."

"But, sir, I was anxious to keep that tooth."

"That was impossible. It is black and decayed. Besides, you have none but old stumps in your mouth; you must get rid of them as soon as possible."

"Mercy! but what shall I have to chew with then?"

"I will put you in a complete set with which you may masticate the hardest food, and which will make you look ten years younger."

Superb! I rush off to find Caroline. She's in the upstairs bathroom, mending the lavatory cistern for the TV journalist. I must say she's very persevering. She's taken off the lid, and has her arm in the water and is fiddling about.

I read it out to her while the lavatory gurgles and splashes. When I come to the end of it, she pulls the plug as a finale and the water jumps up at us. Splosh!

We spring away from it panting. Caroline says:

'But seriously, you'll have to go to Dr Purzelbaum.'

'Oh no!' I'm horrified.

'You will, you know. There's no one else on the island.'

'It's not that bad.'

'Look seriously, Mimi, you can't marry Beetle with none but old stumps in your mouth!'

I fall down on the journalist's bed, suffocating with mirth. Caroline holds on to the wall.

I kick about, shouting:

'But he'll *get* me!'

'Of course he'll *get* you. He's just a lovable old goat.'

'With his bedroom eyes! . . . What are bedroom eyes?'

'Dull, brown eyes with no backs to them.'

'No. It's a sort of yellow lion-iris.'

'Well, he'll turn his irises on you. And don't forget the bag.'

'The bag. What bag?'

'His trousers. Waiting for the birth of Mahomet.'

That does it. The noises I'm making aren't fit to be heard. Do hope Restituta's out in the garden. It's made up partly of fear, this laughter of mine, because Dr Purzelbaum, Dr Oskar (Vespasian) Purzelbaum, *is* funny and also very frighting. He's Viennese, very tall and lanky, wears all his clothes as if they were pyjamas, seduces *everyone*, is always telling you how to behave, making dramas out of nothing and then cashing in on them. He has to *possess* everyone. Ugh! And the awful thing is, one gets rather fond of him. He wears a hearing aid which squeaks when he turns it up: 'Eeko!' So although he's a figure of fun, his unpredictable temper and his knowledge, which is huge, make him dangerous. He runs the thermal baths on Livone. There's a dental department; you can also have massage (half body or whole) and electric shocks. You get psychoanalysed anyway, whether you want it or not, by Dr Purzelbaum. Also I'm told he's got a way of slapping people when they're naked to test their reflexes, and I imagine this could be highly disagreeable. But his chief passion is the thermal baths. They're laid out in the open air and indoors and they all have interesting shapes, kidney, oval, serpentine. Hot bathwater, green, buoyant, mineral and thick, fills them; it's piped out of the volcanic mountainside. As the baths get hotter they become smaller in size. The hottest of the lot is tiny and raised up in somewhat the fashion of a throne. There's a notice about only going in under medical supervision. Some people have heart attacks simply while reading the notice, and inhaling the steam. Purzelbaum is said to prescribe it for his enemies; when you look over the edge, a human head with thermal water up to its neck looks back at you, dreamily. Later you hear that the bather had a coronary, passed out, and had to be fished for with a bright green nylon net like a lacrosse stick.

Then there's the mud. If Purzelbaum doesn't kill you with his baths, he'll do it with his mud. There are unpleasant-looking bathrooms with the locks on the *outside* of the doors. This is to divert the attention of mud-maniacs who might lock themselves in and die, happy and smothered with hot mud. No, they lock you in from outside, and then fill the bathroom up with steam (having laid you out on a perfectly vile truckle bed with a sort of rubber shimmy-sheet on it, indicating they suspect you of bed-wetting to begin with). When they cake you with mud, *they* use rubber gloves (someone's afraid of getting burnt?) and top the whole thing up with dirty white bath-towels. If you have a fit of panic and start calling out, and even get up and beat on the door with your fists, naturally there's dead silence and no one comes. At last, Purzelbaum appears, six foot four inches tall, unlocks the door, insults you, and locks it again.

People come from all over the world for this sort of thing. It's extremely popular with Germans. *'Das ist gut,'* they say, doing slow-motion breaststroke in the large pools or sitting about in their long striped bathrobes, beaming and smiling. They seem to get enormous benefit from it ... Then why does it seem faintly nauseating to me, like having a bath at home at three in the afternoon (Bonnard's mistress), or going to the cinema at eleven in the morning? Is it the combination of pleasure and medicine, a seraglio and a VD clinic? No: possibly just too much hot water all over the place. One thing is certain, it's a very good way to test a man. If he's a capitalist flesh-pot, crazy for luxury, he'll dive straight in. If he's an imitation George Orwell (and they all are nowadays), he won't. Look out, Beetle!

Oh well, I'd better go down to the beach.

3

There are about seventeen umbrellas on the fine white sand. Under each is a family with its equipment. Anyone sunbathing out in the open is young or poor or hunting. You never see men or women oiling one another, down here. All sunbathers are experts who prepare their bodies in advance with white of egg and compose themselves in haughty, classical postures.

Everything is just as I remembered it. The water, much less wet than around the English coast, hardly moves. There are some ripples where it touches the sand. Nothing is too hot. No one talks about the weather. No one reads a book. What for – when everyone here already has a past (even at twenty), and far too many thoughts to think? Except Caroline's children. They have territorial problems. It takes them twenty seconds to sum up a beach and decide on the exact position in the sand which will give them the maximum advantage over everyone else. Their snobbery is faultless. Life on the beach with them is like housework or skiing; you've got to think the whole time.

Caroline says:

'Who was the boy you were talking to?'

Tim, aged nine, answers with disgust:

'That's Dirty, the piazza boy.'

We look across the sand. Dirty is staring at us.

'But why is he called "Dirty"?'

It turns out he plays foul, i.e. kicks you in the behind when you turn round, trips you up, and tries to make you play wheelbarrows upstairs.

'And who's the boy with him?'

Shouts of laughter.

'Oh, that's *Filthy*.'

'But why "Filthy"?'

More laughter, and some shame.

Filthy is backward, and has been seen asleep with his head on the table, and potato crisps sticking out of it, during a meal. Also he growls.

'And that rather nice woman who's smiling at you?'

'That's Filthy's mother.'

James and Ossie (short for Osyth) are working hard in the sand. They're making an effigy. Presently they dress it with bathing trunks and dark glasses. It has red hair (Caroline's head scarf) and is of Daniel Cohn-Bendit. James gives us the gossip off-handedly as he gets on with it:

'D'you know who's at the pensione, upstairs with a private bathroom?' He plumps up one arm.

'No. Who?'

'Mrs Madeline Voos.'

'La Prostitutess!' whispers Caroline to me, all agog. 'She must have come to marry Rupert again!'

'Oh, I can't wait to see her, she's so reassuring. Carol, isn't it a miracle to be back here? I thought the "Yes, darling" days were over for ever.' (They are really. In the old days Prostitutess used to say 'Yes, darling' to people if she couldn't speak their language.)

'She simply *must* marry him this time. Let's get him on to KH3, the rejuvenating drug.'

James, who has overheard, says:

'De Gaulle's on it.'

'Then they'll never devalue. I must tell Killi.' And to me, more secret whispering: 'I say, Mimi, Rupert and she can have fabulous middle-aged sex. Beautiful plump middle-aged bodies, struggling on sofas. I'm told it's like that. People being kind to one another and making love terribly well. You see, you have to go on living and fulfil a young imagination. And a middle-aged imagination. And then an old imagination.'

'Oh, I'm so glad. Actually when I began to make love I simply didn't know what to do next. I knew it was up to me to do something, but *what*?'

'I had the same feeling when I went into the women's lavatory at my first dance. I couldn't think of anything to do. Do come down here and talk into the end of the towel, the children are trying to listen in.'

'She'll give him back his manhood. She even gives me back my womanhood. Still, she mustn't wear him out, otherwise there'll be no tea-parties.'

'How long do things go on when you're middle-aged?'

'It's all a matter of size. The bigger the man the longer it goes on. Shh! What are the children doing?'

'They're interviewing one another. James has invited the French student leaders down to take the waters here.'

'OK. Fine . . . Yes, the size question. And women too, I suppose. La Prostitutess is quite large, with that Pompadour double chin (which is really pretty) and her pekinese. And her bosom too – very luscious, just as though it hasn't been used! But I'm not sure that Rupert likes clasping big women . . .'

'Well, someone's got to clasp them.'

'Ha-ha.'

'She'll be down on the beach at any moment, so we can measure her.'

James walks closer to us on his sandy knees and says:

'I've got a ruler with me, if you want it accurately.'

'James, have you been listening in?'

'No.'

'Well, how did you know what we were saying?'

'You raised your voice at the end,' James says coldly. 'Ossie could tape measure her, if you don't want my ruler. It's nearly worn out from being "zinged".'

'I should have thought you were too old to zing rulers.'

'Tim had it last term and he zinged it to death on his desk.'

'I didn't!' says Tim, growling cheerfully at Filthy over his shoulder. 'I was so bored last term, I used to sit for hours getting the dirt out of the ridges in my desk with the thick part of pen-nibs.' His eyes are like two little goose-berries with joy at the thought of it. 'You've got to get a whole long piece of dirt out in one go, without breaking it.'

'And just as you're getting it, someone comes and jogs your elbow,' says Ossie, with a good memory for suffering.

'It's a microcosm of the real thing.' Caroline is gloomy.

'We could get her on the scales in the piazza' (James is going to inherit all Killi's qualities; already he's thorough). 'After dark,' he adds, kindly.

'If she's overweight, we pack her off to Purzelbaum's to reduce.'

'Nonsense.' I look around at the guilty faces. 'She's perfect as she is, I'm positive. And if anyone's going to reduce her, Rupert will.'

'She's coming down!' James never misses a movement on the beach. He looks at his watch. 'Twelve-forty-five. Five hours until sunset.'

The children are all pointing in the same direction like red setters.

'She's got tons of dung and rubble.' This is James's expression for a woman with more than one handbag.

There in the distance, sinking into sparkling hillocks of sand as she walks, laughing amiably to herself when she does something ungraceful, is plump, edible, golden Prostitutess. Already she has had a long and interesting life, due to the fact that she's always ready to begin a new one. She re-invents herself once a year in the spring; she does not know that she is middle-aged. And yet she knows enough to get rid of those mannerisms very young pretty women adopt when they are being watched and want to have amusing things to do with their fingers. She has style, Italian style, in everything, whether it is beginning a letter or leaning over to switch out the bedside lamp when she's said good-night to you and you're reluctant to leave her room because of the green alabaster pots of make-up and the musical box with a pair of diamond ears on the lid. She's good at life, kind to herself and others. She learned all about massage from a Bengali and is said to have given Rupert a 'rub-down'. Rupert is her Englishman, and if he isn't too spiky this time, she'll probably marry him. My

Aunt Evie is very fond of her. She's pushing of course, but then she has to be.

Yes, under her umbrella it's already Paris. That rose-coloured towel is the size of a bed and much more comfortable than anyone else's. There are cushions, purple ones, and a transistor radio too small to do more than spit or tinkle. She's smoking. What nice round arms she has, with dimples in them. Ha-*ha*, busy with the body milk already. And there goes the peke, fussing over itself, a bogus promenade of ten stamping paces: very masculine . . . The beach-boy seems to be digging Prostitutess a shallow grave nearby . . . Got it! She's going to have herself buried in the shimmering warm, radio-active sand. Prostitutess is the sort of woman who makes land, sea and air yield up to her their benefits, and *at once.* She's only been here ten minutes, but she's remembered the special qualities of the sand. She'll emerge from it *tingling* with new life, even if it's no good at all. Then we'll all have to do it, to catch up.

The children seem to be drifting in her direction. They're armed to the teeth with their squid-hunting gear to impress her. Ossie won't even paddle without a knife and belt around her waist these days. Dirty and Filthy are worshipping, prostrate.

Rupert's TV man has arrived and is hell. He starts by complaining about his bed and calls out: 'I want to complain to the management.' 'We are the management,' says Caroline and myself. 'So what?'

Then we catch him trying to move the dining-room table into his room. This table has a marble top and seats eight. He says there is no table in his room the right height to type on. Then he's mad to know what school Killi went to. At first Caroline and I can't think of any schools at all, finally we think of one to please him, and he's mad with joy because it isn't a very good one, and goes into his room and types solidly for two hours like a machine-gun while Caroline is trying to give a tea-party. When he comes out, she says she's made a mistake. His cough is eight times as loud as I remember it, and goes off every thirty seconds. Kahk-kahk-kahk! He flirts with Restituta and goes to the lavatory every twenty minutes while she's here and calls it 'the loo', consequently the lavatory cistern has bust forever. And we're there all day (or rather every twenty minutes) with our arms in the water trying to get the rubber valve to hold. Not content with Killi's school (the wrong one), he got hold of Caroline's age, thirty-six, from her passport, and armed with these two bits of information he's ready for any conversation, like a ferret carrying a bag of stones all ready to throw at you. He grabs the milk-jug, saying: 'Is this for me?' and pours his coffee out of the jug while you're still carrying the tray, saying: 'I hate cold coffee.' And you should hear him ordering a meal in Italian! Talk about *bel canto*! (In fact he drives you to this sort of pun.)

I suppose this is only the honeymoon which is the prelude to a life-long friendship, but he is making the Italian days prosy. Luckily, Caroline and I can run him down to one another, then we each feel sorry and have to go and make it up to him. The children have started coughing and pressing imaginary lavatory buttons. (I forgot to mention he sings *The Donkey Serenade* with 'effects' in the bathroom, in a dreadful flat humming voice. Honestly, one might as well be in Margate.)

We are all getting rather down in the mouth. He asked Restituta the meaning of some mysterious Italian word he'd got written on a piece of paper and she went off into hysterical laughter and wouldn't tell him. So he showed it to us: '*dablusci*'. We looked it up, but it wasn't in the dictionary. Finally, Caroline got it and started to laugh too.

I'm the only one wandering around who doesn't know what 'dablusci' means. Evidently it's something suggestive, possibly to do with underwear. Perhaps it's the Italian slang for brassière. 'He clawed at her dablusci until it came loose-ee.' Caroline's got a very pretty bra with rosebuds on it, hanging on the chair in her room.

'Why don't you put it away?' I say.

'I'm airing it.'

'God, does it need that much airing?'

No, I give up. That puts me in the same category as the TV journalist. Perhaps I'd better take the descant to *The Donkey Serenade*.

I must clean myself up for Dr Purzelbaum. I'm due there at three-thirty this afternoon. Purzelbaum always gives women appointments at that time so as to prevent them getting a siesta, then they arrive tired and yawning and are more than ever at his mercy. He becomes enraged at the thought of people getting more sleep than he does, and he'll do anything to prevent it. Just like a woman, he lies habitually about the number of hours he's had. 'Only four hours last night,' he'll say with his Sir Thomas More look, as fresh as a daisy. And his patients crawl away, worn out after eight hours' sleep, and cut themselves down to six. If only they knew that he sits on his terrace in the morning and counts up on his fingers, one by one, to make sure he's had his full stint of nine hours before he decides he's in a good temper. Even then things are a bit dicy – if he thinks he's lain awake in the night for a vague, muddled three-quarters of an hour, he's got an excuse for slapping someone down at the baths during the morning (Rupert told me all this).

Anyway, I may not see Purzelbaum at all. I'll get some dental factotum. But just in case, I'd better do something with my hair. Purzelbaum gets fantastically savage if he sees a woman with hair actually *floating* about her face. All great sensualists do. I know, I'll plait this hairpiece and wind it around my head. Then I'll look Bavarian, and Purzelbaum can be Viennese and tap my teeth like a well-mannered fellow countryman.

I plait my hairpiece, and it comes out very thickly and gives me an interesting fat head. I suddenly look prim and good at chess. 'With none but old stumps in your mouth, Brünnhilde, you must castle at once.' Yes, but how can I be sure that marrying Beetle is the right thing to do? Look at Caroline and Killi: snap, snap, snap.

No scent and no lipstick for Purzelbaum. Just your nude maiden mouth. And this long village idiot skirt, so he can't accuse us of bringing our immoral ways to the island with 'mini-cotte'. Purzelbaum doesn't like to think of people marrying, making love, or even holding hands without his permission. Everything has to be sanctified with holy hot water from the thermal baths.

Oh how drowsy it is, with everyone asleep! Doesn't my bed, with its cover of cotton beige look the coolest, most proper spot in the world? Especially with the slatted shadow from one closed shutter falling on it – the colour of well water – and ending up on the marble floor. There's my bedside book, *A Lady's Breviary* by Franz Blei, all the way from the Charing Cross Road with grit and freckle marks in the end papers. And next to it a candle and wax matches, because the lights are always fusing. That extra glass of wine I had at lunch-time is bending me in two; I seem to be anchored to the centre of the earth; nothing matters except the pull of gravity commanding me to be horizontal, in order to digest my spaghetti. Another moment and my body will throw itself down, and I'll push my brow along until it touches the white marble of my bedside table-top (icy), and go off, holding Beetle's hand . . . zzz.

I wait for ages in a tiled salon with magazines and flowers. There's an Isfahani carpet on the tiles; just the thing to make you slip and break your back. Isfahans always look dirty too, due to their delicate colouring. Curious how people like Purzelbaum choose Isfahans, and people like Beetle plum-pudding and elephant's foot.

'It's Mimi!'

'Dr Purzelbaum!'

But he's huge! And all in white, like Everest in overalls.

'My dearest child, so good to see you again.' And he pinches my fingers just as painfully as he did three years ago. I'd better not initiate a conversation; just lie low and see which way the winds blow.

I mount the dentist chair gingerly. My God, I'd forgotten it was made of slimy little leather bolsters. I hold on to each arm. Purzelbaum comes towards me, smiling, and unlocks the fingers I've just locked over the armrests. A bad beginning. My heart made a sudden sideways and upwards movement, which it's never done before. It seems to want to get into my throat. Things start jamming up in my chest after that, and before I can sort them out and quieten them down Purzelbaum is hooking a lint-white napkin under my chin with a little metal hook.

Why is everything always just as you expect it to be?

I start making saliva, I've got nothing else to do. Directly I've made it, I've got to swallow it. Purzelbaum hangs a hook on my mouth, like a coat-hanger; it seems to be sucking my saliva away. Naturally I make twice as much to keep up with it.

Purzelbaum tries to ease my head into the headrest. He winds it up and then down. I look up at him anxiously. The trouble is this Bavarian plait I've got on to please him hurts like hell when he rams it into the headrest. Tears come into my eyes.

'And tell me what has been happening in your personal life all this time?' He has two miniature rolled-up blankets in his tweezers and he puts one on either side of my gum. 'That *is* the spot, isn't it?'

I'm amazed, and gasp out through the cutlery:

'Aah.' (Just like Filthy.)

'Clairvoyant,' says Purzelbaum. 'Like all good diagnosticians, I know a little bit more about you than you know about yourself.'

'Aah.'

'You've been through a very distressing time and you're at the crossroads. You've let your metabolism slip down to a very low ebb.' He suddenly lays the back of his hand, hairy knuckles and all, along my cheek. 'Ah!'

'Aah!'

'Your skin is clammy, my dear girl. That's not right.'

'Naah.'

'If I were a Turkish doctor I would treat your "humour" with warm baths, hot curried food, and a dry warm bed with an electric blanket. That would "dry you out", so to speak. And warm up the soul, the genitals, and the womb.'

Genitals already! It simply takes your breath away; he's like lightning. He'd better keep off my *dablusci*, though with those knuckles of his, or there will be trouble.

(At the word 'genitals' he switched up his hearing aid so that it gave a rusty screech, and stared hopefully at me.)

'Aah.'

He seems dissatisfied, and looks into my eyes. Mine look back, brimming with tears. We stare at one another for a moment. That moustache on his upper lip is a rare object. But no less fierce are the trees forcing their way out of his nostrils down to the brushwood below. He breathes carefully through the trees. I can see every vein on his cheeks and on the end of his nose; amazing, I could draw a map of them in red ink with one of those mapping nibs you use for the Nile delta. Oh yes, I remember that look. In the old days, unless I gave him some big emotion on which he could browse comfortably he would suddenly recall the fact that he was fifty-eight and get up and go. And now he's sixty-one. He certainly won't hang around for snacks. He turns away with the same abrupt move-ment from the past: (Oh well, if you're not going to split!)

But he's back with that wicked tool with a little

Z-shaped leg at the bottom of it. Bold as brass, he inserts a large index finger into my mouth and yanks it into a letter-box shape with extreme brutality.

'Aah!'

'What is it?' He pretends by being over-solicitous that he really cares for my discomfort.

I try hard:

'Na-hing.'

'What, my dear?' He turns his really noisy crackling deaf ear towards me. He even takes the coat-hanger out of my mouth and waits for me to form some sort of reply. I'm being made to seem an idiot. But he *did* pull the skin of my face so hard that for one moment I thought he'd force my nose off its cartilage and I'd never get it back again. I try to smile with a great india-rubber mouth:

'It's just that' (smiling awkwardly) 'I'm always afraid' (hopeless india-rubber plea for mercy) 'you'll pull my nose out of the true.'

'Out of the *what*!'

So it's war! My tears dry up on the spot. I'm seized by a raging hatred, hot enough to warm up two sets of souls, genitals *et al.* Just wait till I get out of this chair. Torturer! Bully! Hateful despot! Rabid puritan bull! Barrett of Wimpole Street!

He scrapes, he pulls my face, he drills, he questions. But it's *too late.* I've turned my whole body into a sort of arrogant elastic. I don't care. I sneer at him. I no longer sweat. My eyes become slits: through the slits, I survey him, inkily. So this is what happens to a man when he gets an inflated idea of his own importance! I know now that hard-bitten gangsters have flesh like mine. And as they look upon their enemies through lids of lead, they usually hum inside themselves a cheap ditty indicative of their massive scorn. *'Is-you-is, or is-you-ain't, my baby?'* I ask Purzelbaum with my eyes. *'Is-you-is, or is-you-ain't, my girl?'* Adding mentally 'Old Filth' as a final insult.

I don't have to tell you that Purezlbaum thrives on this. He becomes friendly and eager to please. If I slobber and don't give a damn, he gently and humbly mops up my chin with the stinking lint-white napkin he hung around it in the first place. And so we go on, until it's all over.

Then when he's unchained the lint-white napkin and is just taking a breath in order to say: 'There! It wasn't so bad, was it?' I get straight up and stretch, *fully.* I then remove all the pins binding the false braid to my head, lift it off, and run my free hand several times through my own hair until it's all over my face like a great big mop. Hooray!

4

Killi is here; he arrived by helicopter, looking tense, up to date, and burnished by the silver dirt of expensive travel. Beetle comes this afternoon, by boat. Oh Beetle! We've used up all our first outrageous kind of joy in one another, and have passed on to a deeper, sweeter drink. I'll hold his ears and eat my way over his features with repetitive Italian kisses. Meanwhile I'm trying to improve my face before he arrives; I want to get it smaller and neater. And I'm perfectly certain I close my jaws on the skew ever since Purzelbaum made my mouth into a letterbox ('Will you have the kindness to tell me where is a box of letters?'). I've spent all the morning swimming fiercely along with my head under water, to wash away the memory of that afternoon. Consequently my head now feels as strong and as tight as a nut. I've got such an appetite I could fall upon a laid-up table, gobble the napkins and etceteras and gnaw a bit off the wooden top while waiting for the meal to arrive. It's something to do with Purzelbaum, because after five minutes' conversation with him you feel so tired you have to go away and cut yourself a piece of cheese and just wolf it down.

There goes Killi, needling Caroline. He puts the whole

authority of his position in the European financial world behind the most piffling domestic comment. He's so used to scoring off business opponents, he can't resist scoring off his wife. His psychology is perfection. In an instant he sees the advantage or disadvantage to himself of every situation which occurs during the day. For example directly the clock ticks past 1.15, lunch is late, and he automatically adds on ten minutes when reminding Caroline of this. As his watch is five minutes fast anyway it means it's already 1.30 when it's 1.15. Puzzling. Then there are the 'friends' and 'workmen'. If a workman comes to mend the lavatory cistern at 1.15 (and remember this is Italy and they always do) Killi goes and has a long slow conversation with him, so as to make lunch even later than it was. Then, white and martyred at two o'clock, he can refuse to eat anything at all. A clear win for Killi.

Ditto Caroline's friends.

If Caroline asks nebulous acquaintances in and they laugh and enjoy themselves, he says: 'I feel like a visitor in my own house.' If she doesn't ask anyone, he says: 'We never see anybody.' If *he* asks someone he says: 'I'm ashamed to ask people, the way we live. There was a hole in the corner of the tablecloth.' 'Nonsense,' says Caroline, 'that's lace. It's got to start somewhere.'

When he's in these moods, he's always doing good deeds around the house, to pile on the agony. He tries to do something rather beneath him, which could be done by Restituta, such as cleaning out the open winter fireplace. It's fatal to be caught 'reading' on such days; it's safer to get up and dust the end of your nose as Killi passes. Caroline has an old sock on a darner which she darns concentratedly for about two minutes as Killi crosses a room. And to round off these moods at such times he fails to communicate his arrangements or his preferences but expects you to know his mind since he knows it so well himself. He sits there in silence and gives the impression of being buried in sand. Or he uses mysterious phrases which have Caroline bewildered for up to eight hours afterwards, such as 'I leave people to draw their own conclusions,' or 'you made it perfectly plain' about the way she greeted someone on the beach, probably a deck-chair boy to whom apparently she was able to indicate in a split second a great chunk of information unfavourable to Killi.

While Killi is using up so much energy in this way, slanting information, walking away from lunch-tables, and generally putting everyone else in the wrong in order to get good marks for his psyche as he moves it over some ghostly chessboard, he gives himself the most awful head-aches. 'Another twenty-four hours,' says Caroline to me. 'He's not himself. He thinks I'm a bank in Brussels. He'll be as right as rain the day after tomorrow.' And the day after tomorrow Killi wakes up perfectly normal, and you wonder what all the fuss has been about.

Curious how some men have to go around making emotional jam out of their families before they can get back on good terms with the world again. It can be awkward when Caroline has something really important to say to him about the children. Then she has to watch him like an embattled fortress and rush up and poke a letter through the slits when the gunfire stops for a moment. Still, Caroline understands him very well and the kind of man-woman game they play seems to suit them. Caroline says with amusement: 'You know, I think Killi must have found that pornographic book I was keeping in my work-basket because he's taken *his* pornographic book away from its hiding place under his trade journals!'

It wouldn't do for me, but then only Beetle would.

I've gone to the port to meet him. I'm dressed in the island uniform: bleached, patched trousers and a pink stretch top. My nails are absolutely clean, and I've made them oval with an emery board. No white flecks on them, thank heavens. I can't remember whether these come from a bad diet or bumping into things. My hands have a tendency to get hot and make veins. I'm afraid Beetle may have noticed this already, but now that they're turning amber and taking up new positions on the ends of my arms, due to days of rest, he could be fooled into thinking them elegant.

5.45 p.m. It's very theatrical with the boat entering this little port and swirling itself around in the beautiful tinted washing-up water. You could get the whole thing – boat, port, quayside, house, Beetle waving on the deck, and myself – on to the stage at Covent Garden.

My love for Beetle swells up inside me. I long to give him back all the good things he's given me. Why, just think that a year ago I couldn't enjoy anything, couldn't stop to stroke a dog or think a thought, above all couldn't grow older because I hadn't loved and been loved in return. I remember kneeling down by my bed with 'flu that winter, alone and in despair, and praying for a lover I could love and who would love me back. And I got Beetle! What good luck. As a little girl I used to dig my forehead into the wool blanket of the bedside to make the prayer 'take'.

Can't remember whether I went through the full magical routine to gain Beetle. Still, as Rupert said: 'It's a pity to miss Italy for a loaf of bread and an orangeade,' meaning don't do anything to lose the prize. And by the same token, do everything to gain it. And Beetle is certainly worth some blanket-rash on the forehead. These Christian routines I've adapted to my pagan superstitions make life a great deal more interesting on a rainy winter's day.

There he is! Beetle is *not* too smooth to wave. He waves and waves like a windmill. That lightweight grey flannel suit is a French dream of springtime; not a sign of his lumpish Cambridge clothes. What's this? Navy-blue silk shirt and tie to match. Must be from Mr Fish: my influence, do hope I'm not ruining a good man.

'Ha-ha! Is that you?' I rush up and stare at him. His eyes pour light down into mine.

'No, I'm you. All brown and dressed in a luscious pink top.' He kisses me on the mouth, quickly and very nicely, because he reckons it's correct for lovers to do what lovers do. If you start pecking people on the cheek, it can go on like that.

'You're so elegant, I hardly dare to touch you.'

'Don't worry. You should see my handkerchief.' Beetle fishes a dreadful yellow rag out of his pocket, and quickly closes his fist over it. 'God! I haven't seen it in the daylight before.'

'It's fantastic. I've never seen anything like it. If I were to starch it and pass it across the counter of the Banco di Napoli, we'd probably get change for trenta-mila lire.'

I take his hand, which is chilly from travelling, and lead him away quickly to the Seicento. Motorcars point in all directions; little children, dogs, men and women, all have equal authority in the traffic and use it. The jam clears so fast that Beetle is amazed. He turns round to look back.

'Do you know that in London it would have taken twenty minutes to clear that road?'

'Straight from the land of cabinet pudding and brown windsor soup!' I bring it out like a mocking bird. 'Down here we're all quick, flowing, gay, and full of genius.'

Beetle, with a really enchanting note of disapproval, says:

'You know I've always adored the Italians.'

'Oh! Beetle! I *love* you. You think they're foreigners. How English. How masculine.'

I've made him look ridiculous, and he waits while I pass a difficult car on the mountain road, and then sings in a contented nationalistic tone, pompous and snorting:

' "No more filthy bread and butter, no more breakfasts from the gutter".'

'Hey, do look at these scab marks on my toes. See them? Those are my summer wounds. I'm hardening the skin between my first and second toes so that I can wear anything.'

'Let me see . . . Hmm, the best scab marks I've seen this year. With scab marks like those you'll have every man south of Rome after you.'

'Will I? What about the ones north of Rome?'

'Don't be greedy.'

'Beetle, what do you count as a pass?'

'Any unnecessary physical contact is a pass,' says Beetle importantly, admiring me as I drive and gently touching the leg nearest to him, just to reassure himself that it's there and is mine.

'Darling, did you have a good flight?'

'Yes thanks. Except that the woman next to me burst into tears when the plane took off.'

'Oh poor thing. It could have been Caroline or me.'

'I know.' After a pause. 'She wasn't English.'

'Who never misses a trick!'

Beetle laughs out loud with joy at being appreciated. I expect we shall play this 'up the English' game for two or three days. I think of another variation on it, and as we turn down into a marvellous valley filled with rose-golden light and a hundred varieties of rainless clouds, all moving peacefully nowhere and glowing like Titians, I murmur:

'Gregorio!'

'Caterina.'

'What did you do to the poor thing in the plane?'

'Gave her my trenta-mila lire.'

'Beetle, when I'm with you I'm so happy it jumps out of the end of my nose. It's simply awful.'

'*Another* reason for having a good strong handkerchief with me!'

'Tell me, how is everyone back in London? I suppose it's the same mud-puddle full of flatfish and newts?'

'More or less. People being lived by their lives.' He says it without regret or grim humour; on the contrary, it sounds amusing. And to me, with real tenderness:

'And how have you been, darling?'

'Fine, thank you.' I immediately feel like crying. I find I'm husky, as though someone's put a wooden tongue in my throat to make it into a flute. 'Actually I do tend to do about an hour's noisy crying every morning due to my mother's death.'

He thinks deeply, with his chin dropped down on his chest.

'You will feel this for a very long time. And we must talk about it together. But, you know, everyone's got to die, *you've* got to die, and it would be a very overcrowded world if people didn't die. It's the ones who are left alive after a death that suffer. The dead don't suffer.'

I'm at once greatly comforted. There are so many stages in grief. One goes through the first layer of events more or less in one piece due to being stunned, only to drop into a great hole in which one realises, apparently for the first time, that death is *final.* And having crawled out of that, and patched up one's manner, the main job is not to slip back into it. Because the sides are so slippery, and like an idiot you forget sometimes that it's there – I mean things seem so normal. When Beetle makes obvious comments he knows that I need to be shown my own events, just like a tourist, since I'm in danger of getting lost inside them. There are people who shake their heads and turn away, saying: 'It's only self-pity, you know, to cry over her.' What they mean is: you're boring. I cry twice as long and loudly in that sort of company, sobbing like a dog.

But in Beetle's company I feel as though I've been re-tuned and call out:

'Fingernails!'

'Black. I know. And my fingers are like black bananas.'

'Aren't people's fingers terrible?'

'Unspeakable. The only fingers worth knowing about are lovers' fingers. Tell me who's here.'

'Killi's here. Morose, virile, pessimistic and expecting nothing from life except money.'

'I like Killi. But he's never grown up emotionally. Only financially.'

'He can't afford to grow up emotionally. It would ruin his business psychology, which is instinctive and fool-proof. The day he gives up his tantrums, Caroline will have to get a job.'

'How's Rupert and the food situation?'

'Not bad at all. La Prostitutess is here.'

'Who's she?'

'The cat's mother. She's down on the beach every day purring in an off-the-shoulder bathing costume. It's the toilet of Venus. She feeds grapes to Rupert, and he snaps his teeth over them like a lion gobbling earrings.'

'Grapes? I can't live on grapes. They're supposed to be there anyway.'

'Yes, well, she never wastes anything. Not even her dreams. And, surprisingly enough, they're quite interesting. I followed her example and had a dream the other night. And do you know, Beetle, it was such a dirty dream that when I woke up I was quite shocked!'

'Teaching you to have dirty dreams, is she!'

'The children love her. Ronald Dyson, our lavatory man, carries her bag and beach stool. Killi carries her peke. She says: "Men hate to be adored. Make them your slaves!"'

'She needn't try to charm me,' says Beetle gruffly, half charmed already.

'Oh, I forgot. We've got an admirer with perfectly white hair who follows us about. Every time Killi lies down to sunbathe, he crawls into our sandpit and tries to get to know him. If Killi goes for a swim, he swims after him and tries to say jolly things in deep water. The children follow him on a lilo, armed to the teeth, looking for squid.'

'Does he look like a squid?'

'No. He's really rather good-looking, and extremely polite and friendly. The only trouble is he gave us four biscuits on the train during the revolution, and Killi's furious, and keeps swimming away from him, and says he made him lose a flipper on some rocks by coming up behind him in the sea and saying: "I want to discuss the French franc with you." And Killi says his white hair makes him sneeze anyway.'

'I'm surprised he didn't lose both flippers.'

'And, Beetle, I went to Dr Purzelbaum.'

'What for?' he asks suspiciously; he's heard of the famous Purzelbaum.

'Wonky tooth. I was afraid you'd say: "Stand back! Your breath is – oh *dio!*"'

'Exactly what I was going to say. Delicious. It's the best breath there is. Can we stop so that I can taste it?'

'Woops!' I jolt the car, and stop.

We touch one another and go on a short journey. In the middle we say 'Hullo' to one another helplessly, for fear of getting lost. What strong grey flannel arms. I shall never be cured of them. We kiss so well, without meaning to, that Beetle again laughs out loud for joy. Oh he's so triumphant! It's like a cock crowing. And I'm delighted with him; his strong neck so well rooted and bolted into his shoulders (always a point on which I'm vulnerable. Woe betide those with weedy necks), his silky young hair that smells of lemon, the layers of imagination and intelligence inside his kissing mouth, with all its moods and always its fastidiousness. The basis of my happiness lies in the right-ness of his attitudes to life and to women: if these are faulty, a woman can never be herself in that man's company, which means she can never be truly sensuous. For no woman will show herself *as she is* to an enemy; and so men who prey on women for sex, or money, or children, or introductions, or to gain identity, will always say as a matter of pride that they have never been in love, have never found anyone their equal, and consider the gulf between the sexes unbridgeable, due to the fact that they have carefully removed the trust on which a natural rela-tionship could develop, in order that this should be so.

The women they do gain over are always on guard, sparring with them, deeply unhappy and suspicious.

We're all going to have tea with Rupert. Caroline and I walk up together. Ron Dyson has gone on ahead so that he can tell everyone Caroline's age and which school Killi didn't go to. Caroline is looking ravishing in a blouse of the same material as her *dablusci*. She's got a bigger, more hard-wearing body than I have, and I've secretly begun doing exercises to get mine up to the same standard.

When we arrive there, David Rety, Rupert's other jour-nalist, has made tea and apparently made it all wrong.

'There was an old packet of workman's Typhoo tips which I brought over in '66 . . .' Rupert is going on like this in a grumpy voice.

I take one sip and put my cup down.

'Oh, God, he's made it with workman's bits.'

Beetle makes choking laughter. He says:

'We could water the garden with it, but only certain beds.'

Waterloo Barns, the American who keeps a library on Livone, says:

'It's delicious. I'm beginning to believe in things again.'

Caroline says:

'It really is the vilest, murkiest stuff I've tasted for a long time. Thank God we've got tea-bags.'

'Oh I think tea-bags are *low.*' That's Dyson. He really is making himself popular. Caroline and I both stare at him and he stares back. I can feel Carol nearly writhing with fury on the sofa beside me. Does he think we don't know tea-bags are low? Of all the people in the world most calculated to know that sort of thing, Caroline and I are the ones. Whereas he . . . is practically a tea-bag himself. Naturally we've got to defend tea-bags now; curious how a conventional English animal like Dyson forces you to see the genius of Italian domestic life. Caroline paints a calm and radiant picture of herself making tea in a German porcelain teapot, day after day, with tea-bags.

'It was probably the German porcelain that made it drinkable.'

At which Caroline turns to Rupert and says:

'Shall we water it down? Ronald has kidney trouble, you know.'

'Have I?'

'Yes,' I say firmly, 'you most certainly have. You really ought to go and see Dr Purzelbaum, Ronald. Because it's spoiling your complexion.'

Caroline wants to congratulate me.

'He's got a wonderful new Turkish cure for every sort

of disease,' I go on kindly. 'No matter how private. You don't want to take that sort of thing back into the English countryside, do you?'

'What's wrong with me for God's sake?'

Caroline stands up and pours her tea over the balcony.

'My God,' says Beetle, 'I hope it doesn't kill the flowers.'

'Mine's got grease spots on it,' I say, interested. 'Another cup please.'

Rupert isn't really paying attention; he keeps looking up, as though expecting someone who's late.

Now Waterloo Barns is a great peacemaker, and he can see the tea-bag thing is getting nasty.

'When you arrived,' he says pleasantly, 'we were just talking about Lytton Strachey.'

'Oh good idea!' I get pink. 'I'll be Carrington. Would you like to be Lytton, Rupert?'

'Oh, he never says anything.'

'Yes, but he makes up for it by having a beard.'

'Could someone make Rupert a beard?' asks Caroline. 'Then Mimi can go and sit on his knee.'

'Carrington never sat on Lytton's knee!' Rupert is quite shocked. Dyson and Rety look upset too. They all guard Lytton Strachey, frowning at us from the white cliffs of Dover, outraged to think of his homosexuality being impugned in this way. But Beetle is already back with some thick sprigs of rosemary; he makes them into a first-class green beard, all prickly and scented.

Rupert, who really is a duck, puts it on and gives one of his enchanted smiles.

'How do I look?'

'Strachey to a tee! Now just twine your fingers together

so that they look macaroni *al dente,* scribble down *Eminent Victorians,* and you're ripe for Carringtonitis.'

Beetle signals to me: 'Don't go too far!'

'Or wouldn't it be more fun,' I say wickedly, 'if I were Lytton and Rupert was Carrington? Then we'd get it more or less right.'

'No, darling,' says a new, throbbing voice from the doorway, '*I* will be Carrington!'

It's La Prostitutess! A vision in orange taffeta, with her little pekinese lying along her arm, silent, clever and knowing when it's well off. She makes some movements, as though unused to walking (I happen to know that she rises at dawn and walks two miles along the coast every morning simply to clear her complexion). That taffeta rustles like Hawaii in a hot wind.

'Maddy!' Rupert scrambles up, throwing off his beard. All the men half-stand, holding tea-plates to their stomachs, totally unable to fight a woman as obvious as Prostitutess. After all they've only been used to female half-backs, friendly equals they can go for walks with. No such nonsense here. No rights for women and other non-subjects like that. You'd never get Madeleine Voos to admit she could get as far as the piazza alone. She has instant rapport with everyone; this one gets a little pressure of her fingers, that one a twinkling smile; everything she does is interesting. Why is that, I wonder? I suppose because it interests *her.*

'Darling, I was accosted!' she says in thrilling low tones to Rupert.

'No!' Rupert looks stunned, unhappy.

'Yes, darling. I was swimming slowly along in the

thermal baths among the Germans, when a beautiful Persian came and swam along beside me. He said he had been to see Oskar Purzelbaum about his heart, but every time he began to describe his habits Purzelbaum turned off his hearing aid. So I let him describe his habits to me, because he seemed upset.'

'Why should he describe his confounded habits to you!'

'He says he lifts his typewriter over his head thirty times every morning, which is why he looks so young for his age.'

'He doesn't.'

'He says the world of international finance is not run from Trieste or Zurich or Brussels, but from Karachi. And that he is a financial genius but is terrified of having his ideas stolen, which is why he goes about incognito and is faithful to his forty-three-year-old wife.'

'I'm very glad to hear it.'

'He also says, darling, that he has come to do a big deal with Killi because his astrologer told him he would, but that Killi's behaviour is strange.'

Everyone looks at Caroline as though it's her fault. Caroline laughs. She knows perfectly well Killi's behaviour is strange. If the Persian finds it strange, how does he think she, Caroline, finds it? Very strange indeed.

Prostitutess rustles to regain our attention.

'But you are not to worry about it, darling,' she says to Caroline, 'because he *understands* him.'

'But Killi hates that!' says Caroline involuntarily.

'No, darling, you are mistaken. He does not hate it; he loves it. Businessmen make love to one another. You know, they hold each other's hands, they write letters, they make gifts. You know what this Persian has done for your children, darling?'

'No. What?' Caroline's on edge.

'He let them use his phone to phone the students in Paris, and the leaders are coming down for a rest while they negotiate with Pompidou.'

'Killi *will* be pleased.'

'It was a very noble and realistic thing to do,' says Prostitutess, giving her blessing to it.

On the whole, if you're controlling the price of the franc, I suppose it is. And Prostitutess isn't an idiot. In fact, in my mind I can see the two of them conning one another gently as they swim together up the heated kidney pool. But who wins? She says to Rupert:

'Am I doing Carrington nicely for you, darling?'

'Beautifully. But there's a fly in the ointment. Maddy, I wish you wouldn't gossip to *foreigners* when you have your bath.'

'He came to me, like a humble little water-vole, really like an otter, so discreet.'

'One minute he's a water-vole and the next he's an otter!'

'Then you must come down with me, darling, and protect me from these Persian water-voles and otters they have swimming about there with hurt feelings. In fact, you must *all* come.' She's giving it to the journalists and Waterloo Barns now. 'Then we can keep down the water-voles with English dolphins and American whales! Look at me!' (we are), 'I'm cured! It's marvellous. That is what Purzelbaum has done for me.'

'But Maddy, there was nothing wrong with you!'

'That's what I say!' says Ron Dyson, coming up for air with a jerk.

'This is the time to go!' says Prostitutess triumphantly. 'Go while you are still able to go.' (Dyson looks sulky.)

'Maddy, you're too ridiculous for words.'

'I know, darling. But look at the German economy. Booming. And where are all the Germans? In Purzelbaum's baths, as strong as bulls. Even your white-haired little water-vole –' She brings it out *sotto voce* to Caroline.

'He's *not* my white-haired little water-vole.'

'Even he knows where to go for his strength. Look at the British economy. Is it booming?'

'We'll go tomorrow,' says Beetle firmly.

Waterloo Barns, who is really too much of a scholar to get into a bathing costume, is chewing over his new rôle as an American whale. He asks humorously:

'Does it count if Dr Purzelbaum comes into the library to visit me?'

'Please.' Prostitutess seems to be beseeching him. 'Will you take off my shoe? Right off?'

We gaze at her naked foot. It's one of those chubby white feet very young angels have in Rubens' paintings. The small rose-coloured toes haven't a mark on them. Beetle catches my eye, and we both look at Rupert, who seems about to have an orgasm on the spot. Waterloo Barns holds her shoe uneasily, it's so absurd, so much a brand-new golden slipper that's just fallen out of a cracker, that it seems to put all his years of study, all his scholarship in doubt.

Next Prostitutess picks up pieces of paper with her toes. She does it neatly. And her pekinese gets down and plays with her foot as if it was another pekinese. Wuff!

'You see!' she says, active and full of joy.

'You shouldn't do that in public,' says Rupert, an odd healthy red. 'Put it away, Maddy.'

'My economy is booming!' Prostitutess picks them up twice as fast. Honestly she ought to restrain that foot of hers. It looks quite capable of writing a letter or making an obscene phone-call. (Caroline once had an obscene phone-call and says she thoroughly enjoyed it.)

'Maddy!' He takes the shoe away from Waterloo and puts it back on her foot. And high time. We're all tremendously relieved. You need really strong cups of tea if people are going to carry on with their feet like that in public. You see, there's an overwhelming temptation to show what your own can do. I happen to be able to open all my toes sideways, like a hand. But I'm saving it up as a horrible shock for Beetle in private.

'All the same,' Rupert has the last word on Purzelbaum's baths, *'pour moi de l'eau sans mouche.'*

5

I'm in the big kitchen in Aunt Evie's house, getting lunch. Restituta has the day off because it's a holiday. She has so many days off that it's a great treat when she turns up at all. Ron Dyson thinks he's charmed her. Actually she loathes him; and we may lose her altogether if he goes on charming her. I know I shall have to end up by liking this man out of pity. He's like a rough awkward chest of drawers out of the local carpenter's shop; the drawers are all ill-fitting and go kahk-kahk-kahk when you touch them, the rest consists of sharp corners and splinters which have never been bevelled off. What he needs is a female chest of drawers of the same *genre* and then they can go kahk-kahk-kahk together. I think he must be lovable, because he irritates me to screaming point by being awful, and then I feel a wave of affection for him and go and do something to give him pleasure, quite unnecessarily. Caroline is behaving in the same way, so obviously she's not the matching chest of drawers. He's very good with the children in every way, even their snobbery is the same as his, so possibly that's the answer: he won't grow up. David Rety, Rupert's other journalist, looks more rounded somehow, but he's probably doing terrible things up there – who knows if he hasn't actually *got* the dining-room table through the door and into his bedroom? That seems to be the major weakness of Rupert's friends. Even Beetle, can I be sure how Beetle will react to a dining-room table that attracts him? They've all three gone off to the thermal baths, and I'm most anxious to know how Beetle responded to that bestial hot water.

There are blue and white tiles in the kitchen. I've just put a sprig of rosemary into the boiling salted spaghetti water. I can see Dyson's terrible underwear on the clothes-line outside from here, then Killi's, brand-new, then a sort of black rat – oh, one of the children's beach towels. I do hope Beetle's underwear isn't too ghastly. In the clear light down here these things tend to be more important than in England.

Gosh, I know a great deal about Beetle, and I don't come to the end of him. He interests me more today than he did yesterday. I know some of his psychological weaknesses; for example, he likes to be indispensable to the people he's taken a fancy to. When he's with two of them together, his charm is torn in half and he suffers considerably. He's built to satisfy the emotional demands of one person at a time. This seems so honest and straightforward that I can't help liking it. Ah, that's the secret, isn't it? I *like* Beetle, before I love him. We compare notes on every aspect of life, and we agree that everything we were taught as children is untrue. Life *improves* as you go on, and each decade is better than the last. Also I asked Beetle if, when he was alone with his mind, he found that it put him back into a good humour – after a day being battered in London. He said, yes it did. Mine does. But there's always someone like Purzelbaum who growls at you when you're contented: 'You enjoy life too much. It shouldn't be allowed!'

Beetle and I also made the mutual discovery that happiness begins the day you grow up. You learn to grow up, you learn to get over a death, you learn to be sexy, you learn that responsibility can be worthwhile, you learn that you're entitled to your own life.

Our feeling for one another keeps changing. Yesterday I tried to put myself entirely into his position and to take a look at myself from inside his life, to see whether I was adding the right kind of happiness to it. My character, my body, my clothes, my profession, and my emotions all looked very much smaller seen from his life. I was really somewhat touched. Just like a little girl playing with odds and ends. And yet here I am in myself, formidable, foursquare, with an absolute mountain of a past to live off, hundreds of interesting emotions, opinions on everything, long hair to be washed and plaited, and never a dull moment from the instant I jump awake in the morning. I say 'jump awake' because I always know the exact moment I'm awake, and in a split second the relevant information about the position of my bed, the time of day, the country I'm in, my problems, my finances, *and* the humour of it all, opens out in my head. There is no drowsy groping after personality. Now we have a great problem with Killi because he doesn't dream and consequently he never believes he's been to sleep, and never quite knows whether he's awake or asleep. No wonder he has to spend the rest of the day organising people and getting them to jump to it.

What happens if Beetle, who now seems so normal, turns into another Killi? I must say Killi is lamblike at the moment. But that's a week's work by Caroline. And it'll take her another week to get herself un-nagged.

Footsteps. It's Beetle and the other two! They're steaming with rage.

'He insulted us!'

'He didn't!'

'He did!'

'Oh good. Tell me what happened.'

'We all three got into the biggest pool and swam about in the middle. Suddenly a very tall man in drag appeared' (this is David Rety talking) 'with raglan sleeves! Well, he watched us quite silently for a bit, and Ronald called out to me that he had found something at the bottom of the pool –'

'It was a sort of step. I bruised my feet on it.'

'OK. Well, I went over and stood beside him, feeling around on the bottom with my foot, and the man – who I took to be Purzelbaum – came up alongside us and stared meaningfully at us, and I thought he called out: "*Nicht küssen*". Was that what he said?' Rety looks at the others, who laugh helplessly.

' "*Nicht küssen*"!? No kissing!' I can hardly get it out, because that intolerably painful laughter that bypasses the head and goes straight to the stomach like colic has come on and I can't control it for the moment. Ow. It really hurts.

'Well, I could have heard wrong. But that's what it sounded like. You can imagine we were absolutely galvanised. No one said anything. The Germans went on flopping about around us. Finally he said in English: "I'm sorry, I thought you were German." We still didn't say anything, so then he came clean and said were we English and would we care to come and have a cup of coffee with him as the pool was going to be drained?'

'We didn't have much option,' said Beetle.

'So we climbed out, feeling rather cold after that super hot water – no sign of it being drained incidentally – and Ronald started coughing, and I'm afraid I sneezed . . . well, I was chilly.'

'And he pounced on it!' says Beetle.

'He said sneezing had a sexual significance. And he went on to say that everyone brought their sexual problems to Italy to solve. He said you could tell whether anyone had a sexual problem by the way they answered the telephone.'

'Let's ring him up.'

'We're going to. Don't worry. Well, he got us into his consulting room and you can imagine we were at a grave disadvantage standing there in our bathing trunks, shivering while we waited for the coffee . . . And he roamed around in that white robe of his, and explained to us that strictly speaking we should have had a *medical* examination before going into the pool, because it was his duty to make sure people could stand the temperatures. And also he had to be certain that people didn't *abuse* the pool.'

'And what, I should like to know, did he mean by *that*?'

'You're not to bruise the bottom with your feet,' says Beetle, looking at me.

'Then he suddenly turned on poor Ronald –'

'Yes, he buttonholed me!'

'And said something about "Tell me your symptoms. I take it you have some."'

'Yes, exactly. It was terrible.' Kahk.

'Then he pointed to a painting on the wall and asked Ronald if he knew what it was.'

'Patronising old –'

'Exactly. It just so happened that Beetle knew the painting and said it was a . . .'

'A Pontormo. Just a lot of naked, struggling grey bodies.'

'And he asked Ronald: "What light does that shed on life?"'

'I knew it was a trick question like "Have you stopped beating your wife?" so I kept quiet.'

'So he started lecturing us on learning to respect our bodies. He did! Three grown men, standing there in bathing trunks waiting for a cup of coffee they didn't want! He waffled on about bodies. He said you must respect your body whatever it does, even if it lets you down by apparently sordid acts' (guffaws) 'and you must exult in it. He said all Englishmen who exulted in their bodies had to leave England, like Shelley and Norman Douglas! He said Englishmen had great difficulty in forming proper emotional relationships, that is why Britain was leading the world in fashion, in intellectual life, and as a welfare state. Apparently we use all these things to cover up our inability to form relationships.'

'All we were doing was swimming in his idiotic pool,' says Ronald resentfully.

'I suddenly got very angry,' says Beetle. 'I pointed out that we had paid 360 lire each to get into his thermal baths, that there was no notice about medical examinations on that particular pool, and that we were tired and cold and would like to go.'

'That really spurred him into action – the thought that

he was losing us! He apologised profusely, so much so that we had to say: "No, no. Not at all" and so on. He then said that we might be interested to see the breakfast menu of the Rest House at the thermal baths because they did English breakfasts!'

'As though you cared whether they did boiled missionaries!'

'He said they had grilled kidneys, fried baby whiting, fancy bread, compote of prunes, everything! Then he went on to say there was a ping-pong room and a gymnasium where he, personally, took the Hatha Yoga classes.'

'You bet!'

'At that point Ronald suddenly said: "Oh!" It was the first word any of us had managed to get in since the Hatha Yoga tack –'

'Well, I remembered a master at my prep school who used to get into Hatha Yoga positions. The whole thing was thoroughly unpleasant.'

'And Purzelbaum rounded on him and said: "Don't you say 'Oh' to me in that tone of voice."'

'I thought he was going to slap my face!' Kahk.

'So we just walked out,' says Beetle. 'Things had already gone much too far.'

'And he accompanied us to the door talking volubly the whole time. He said how much he had enjoyed the conversation, and that it reminded him of the time he had spent at Oxford after qualifying at Heidelberg. He said that Mrs Voos had mentioned we were here, and what "charmers" we were, but that she, of course, had a very serious problem, because she was a – and here he dropped his voice and hissed – a "rabid brood mare".'

'What's that?'

'Haven't the slightest idea. We thought you might know, Mimi.'

'Me! Certainly not.'

'Well, the way he said it made your blood run cold.'

'Honestly. He's *ruining* Italy.' I frown.

'It was marvellous to get out into the sunshine again.'

'You all look quite pale. What a morning! Listen, the spaghetti's ready and there's the sauce bubbling like blood over there. Beetle darling, if I load up the tray, will you carry it out to the terrace? Don't forget that bottle of Livone. The local wine's excellent, and we'll all be drunk in no time.'

Five minutes later we're sitting on the terrace, very sunny and jolly, each with a *mustacchio* of tomato sauce. These don't make you look beautiful, but somehow they never fail to make you laugh. After one glass of wine, we're carefree and the slightest remark turns into a joke, a pun, with two minutes' worth of permutations.

'The staggering thing about Purzelbaum,' says David Rety, 'is that he does all the things that people have warned you he will do.'

'You mean the whole morning went just as you expected?' Two swigs at my red wine.

'Well, if you put it like that, yes. I would have been awfully disappointed if nothing had happened.'

'He needs to be taught a lesson,' says Ronald Dyson, with considerable authority. After all, he's suffered more than the other two, for whom Purzelbaum was merely a humorous outing. 'In England he'd be struck off the register.'

'He'd never get on it,' says Beetle. 'He needs a register all to himself. It would be in the form of a breakfast menu.'

'It's simply outrageous that he should get away with insulting people like this. He needs direct action. Some unanswerable insult that absolutely flabbergasts him.'

'Yes, leaving him gibbering, totally insane with rage, tearing up telephone directories and drilling his own teeth. A rabid brood mare.'

There's an explosion of laughter after this piece from Rety, who really is turning into a humorist. Dyson beats his glass on the cane chair to get back to normal. Beetle and I keep looking at one another, and that instantly doubles the joke. He wipes his tears away, and asks:

'Well, what do you suggest, David?'

'One of us says: "Mind your manners, Sonny Jim!" and we set fire to his trousers.'

'Superb! It's absolutely infuriating – it's the "Sonny Jim" that does it.'

'He'll simply go black in the face.'

'He'll be black all over once his trousers are alight.'

'He'll have to jump into one of his own pools.'

'We'll drain it first.'

'In case he abuses it.'

'When he calls out "Oh!" we'll say: "Don't you say 'Oh' to us in that tone of voice."'

David Rety stops laughing and a look of revelation passes over his face. With a mad light in his eyes, he calls out:

'I've got it!'

'What? David, quickly!'

'No. This is something real. You know he has a very fine garden in his private house – it's just below Rupert's?'

'Yes. Well?'

'Well, he's got a little lemon tree growing in the middle, which is his pride and joy. Right. We arrange with a local gardener, whom we pay in advance, to go in and cut down the lemon tree and snip off all flower-heads.'

'What reason do we give?'

'Hay fever. The Doctor has developed an allergy to flowers. Lemon trees bring him out in a rash.'

'It's pretty brutal. Should we merely cut off a few branches of the tree?'

'Oh no. It's the whole lemon tree or nothing. Pruning it is positively doing him a favour. It'll sprout more strongly than ever.'

'Hmm! The whole lemon tree. Do you think he'll recover?'

'Of course not,' David Rety is chortling. 'He'll never recover. It'll be the happiest day of his life. He really *will* have a grudge and a good reason for it. If you're going to weaken, think of all the helpless people he's steamed like plaice fillets in those bathrooms of his. Take one look at that nylon net he uses for fishing out harmless victims. Lemon trees are two a penny here. He can replace it tomorrow.'

'I must say, your plan is attractive.' I brood on it.

'It's a genuine effort to right a social wrong.'

'Who does the organising and instructs the gardener?' asks Beetle, and for some reason we all look at Dyson. It's so unanimous that he can't get out of it. He caves in, bleating mournfully:

'Why me always?'

I wonder if I ought to restrain them. What's my

responsibility in Aunt Evie's absence? Am I to protect a Viennese doctor's lemon tree from three English journalists? I examine my own feelings and find that my natural instinct is to go straight round and cut down the tree myself, as a retaliation for Purzelbaum's having made a fool of my gentle and lovable Beetle. That's clear enough. I enter my bedroom, root out the Italian phrase-book from a pile of summer clothes, and ceremoniously hand it over to Dyson. The others are sleeping in the shade in the garden. Beetle looks so young. I return to the bedroom thinking, 'I shan't sleep,' close the shutters and lie on the bed in a non-sleeping position. I fall into deep slumber. Oh – ah! How good it is, how refreshing, excellent, so effortless.

La Prostitutess always has something to do. Today she's trying on hats, seated at the little wooden dressing table in her pensione suite. There's a big jug of roses, wide open but still fresh roses with deep unmarked vegetable velvet on their petals except for the riverbeds of dew and nectar running into their mouths. You breathe them in in amazement, saying to yourself, 'So this is what a Latin rose really is – incredible.' Caroline and I are lolling on the large double bed. It has a white canopy. I'm examining the roses. Caroline is asking Prostitutess questions. She answers:

'Women take their first lover because they think it will help them with their husband, darling. Like this one?' It is a circular cherry-red silk cushion with an aperture for the skull. She gets it on her head with incredible speed; wham! it's on.

'I like it from the front. It looks rather like a cushion from the side. And does it help them?'

'No. It only makes it worse, by showing up the contrast. Going back to your original man is the hardest thing in the world. Only a very skilful and loyal woman can manage it. Green is always very good on the head, like this, but you must get rid of your hair otherwise you look vulgar. But with your hair up, you can look as if your skin is made of green milk.'

'Yum-yum. But what about men? Can't they go back?'

'Yes, they are very good at going back – depending on the man of course. And in fact some of the best men would rather go back than forward, being timid by nature and creatures of habit.'

'So women would rather go on to greener grass, and men would rather go back. I'm surprised they ever meet.' I'm logical at least.

'It is a great mystery, darling. They meet on the way, like trains. You see, it's difficult for women in England at the moment because the men are taking away their gaiety. That is why it is a depressed society. Because in any society it is the women who make the gaiety.'

'But why are the men taking it away?'

'Poor darlings, they don't mean to. It's just that with two wars they have forgotten how to live. And they think that if the women do what they, the men, want, they will be happy.'

'And that's not right?'

'Oh no, darling, never!' Prostitutess looks almost shocked. 'Men do not know what they want, so they can never be happy. Whereas women know exactly what they want, and when they get it they are happy. So, you see, happiness starts with the women. You can never please a man by doing what he wants, never, because he always wants something else immediately after. But if you do what *you* want, and get happiness out of it, then the man catches the happiness from you! It's simple!'

'But women are very accommodating and self-sacrificing –'

Prostitutess lays down in her lap the broad black summer hat with a morsel of tulle, the colour of a bird of paradise, tied around the crown, and says in despair:

'It's tragic! It makes me so miserable. And you see the result when you walk along Knightsbridge, not one contented face!' (We can't help smiling at this minimal piece of market research.)

'But, Maddy, are you telling me I ought to be nasty to Killi?'

'What has Killi been doing?'

'Tantrums, walking away, and nagging about household tasks that aren't his business.'

'You must have an affair! Straight away! He is using you as a therapy, he has forgotten you are a woman.' Shrieks!

I sit up straight and blink. Caroline is making big eyes. Prostitutess doesn't waste any time. She pulls the word 'affair' out of the hat as fast as a conjuror pulls out a rabbit.

Prostitutess looks at Caroline with some speculation, until Caroline catches the drift of her thoughts and snaps:

'No! *No, no, no. Not* my white-haired little water-vole.'

'Waterloo Barns then.'

'No! I like him much too much. He's a duck.'

'A duck is what you need, my darling. No woman can have too many ducks. Waterloo is the only really civilised man on Livone, and I say this to you with my darling Rupert only three hundred yards away. Waterloo is good-looking, amusing, a great Jungian scholar, and may ... even be a good lover.' She says the last few words, weighing them up so carefully, to herself, that I tremble for Waterloo – in case he doesn't quite come up to expectation. Until she adds, out of pure mischief: 'But then, they all think they're good lovers. And I feel like saying, "I could tell you a thing or two".'

'Well, Maddy, you know everything there is to know. Whereas we don't.'

'Then you must *learn*, darling. Unless you have a sexual hold over a man, you have nothing.'

'Oh boo! What about love and friendship?'

'Salt and pepper, darling. But *intelligence* is far more important. There are days when my Rupert does not love me and does not like me. But he always wants my company.'

'That's it,' says Caroline with great interest, 'you have *equal* conversations. Whereas if I discuss anything whatsoever with Killi, he automatically assumes he is right, purely on account of his success in business.'

'Just go out and run up a few bills, darling, for the house, as well as yourself ... some completely useless pillowcases, darling, guest towels embroidered with *his* initials.' She's bewitching with that twitch of a smile which she employs when only using one-eighth of her charm. 'I was advising a girl friend the other day and I said, "Don't cry because you haven't had sexual intercourse with him for five years. Go out and buy yourself a nice coat, not mink because it's so ageing".'

'Actually, pillow-cases are always useful,' I say truthfully, shaking my head.

Caroline is too busy getting the maximum amount of information. After all, she broke off in the middle of a row with Killi this morning, and naturally she's anxious to get back to it with some fresh psychological angles. She moans:

'Killi's always criticising my clothes, and he has awful taste. His idea of a well-dressed woman is a middle-class blonde with hair in fixed curls and a neck which has had the secateurs up it. He calls that "well groomed".'

Prostitutess happens to be combing out her own little blonde head at the moment, and I notice she quickly erases the tighter curls. She says:

'They are all vulgar, that is typical of a nice man, darling. They never have any taste. It's a good test of masculinity. All hairdressers are terrible unless you control them. They will make you into a burning bush or a skinned cat.' She ties a skimpy pink cotton-silk handkerchief under her chin and has a really good look at herself in the mirror. 'Does my nose stick out?'

'No, Maddy, not too much. How can you tell if a man is really stuck on you?'

'Yes, pink is not too bad for noses. It is navy-blue that gives you the Dong's nose. Well, if he's stuck on you he says very passionately, "Oh *you*!" If he says, "Oh, you *darling*," it's only sex.'

'Gosh,' I say, 'then I've had some narrow squeaks.'

'That's right, darling. You go on and squeak. It's quite right for a woman to squeak. Squeaking is pretty.'

'I could squeak until I was black in the face, and it wouldn't make any difference to Killi. If I ask for affection, he looks persecuted. Everything has to be impersonal, otherwise he goes yellow and starts yawning.'

Prostitutess ticks Caroline off:

'You must stop living the Englishwoman's life, darling! They are all slaves at the moment, because they are studying the men and not creating status for themselves.' She taps on the dressing-table with her finger, making a noise like a bird pecking delicately. 'I don't mean a career.' She shakes her head quite violently. 'No, no! In France or Italy women run part of a house, or they serve in a shop, they are nothing, but they make it important and they *possess* it. One of the laws of life is that you must have pride and you must possess something, yourself, or a room, or a house, or a piece of land, or a business. You must give orders, darling, and do what you want to do. Then Killi will be very happy, because it is normal. That is why Rupert adores me, because I make life normal, and he feels safe. You must have a strong life, then Killi will adjust his life.'

Boom! Caroline has really been bombed with information. She's looking silent and wise, so it's all gone home. Killi's down on the beach, trying to get his legs brown; this always takes him ages because they have wool on them and the ultra-violet rays can't get through. By the time he gets back Caroline will be a different woman. She won't study his moods, and if he walks away from the lunch table she'll call out, 'See you at dinner!' and get on with her status. In fact this is a good thing, because this morning when Killi got up he asked us all how we had slept. But we know him far too well to smile in reply and say, 'Very well, thanks,' and so we carefully answered 'So-so. A bit wakeful. Did you hear that dog at three o'clock this morning?' And just as he was looking slightly more cheerful because he hadn't heard the dog at three o'clock (there wasn't one) Ron Dyson came in and said *he'd* slept like a top. Killi promptly turned sour. He's taking some new sleeping tablets and apparently these make him dream he's awake. You can't win with Killi. So Caroline does have a problem.

The curtain of wooden beads across the door of the bedroom-living-room rattle, and in comes the pekinese. Then just above it the beads open and there – talk of the devil again – is Caroline's Persian! He's exquisitely dressed. Dark grey sea-island cotton shirt, lighter grey silk tie and handkerchief with the sheen of good gin. Grey cashmere cardigan. White hair well back, properly cut and greased to follow his skull; lots of it too. Oh – and look at those perfect hands. Narrow brown fingers, covered with unmarked skin like a boy's, and never for a moment unintelligent. He's carrying a big basket, and it seems to be for Caroline because all the passion of a Baghdad night is being discharged across the room to where she sits on the white bedcover, organising Killi's very interesting neurosis. He turns to Prostitutess with the air of having been married to her for about twenty years:

'Three of you together! It's too much. I am blinded!'

'Darling, what is in that basket with all that green grass?' (I like the way she gets down to things.)

'Ah. Well . . .' Mystery. More Baghdad nights. Then a hand goes in and feels around in the freshly-cut green grass. 'I thought I might find the girls with you, this morning, dear Mrs Voos. I had an intuition. And so I came here with my little gift for them. I wanted your approval to be sure that it was the right thing for an Eastern man to give as an act of homage to a Western woman.' That ties up Prostitutess for a second. Now for Carol. 'Do you remember, Mrs Vandeveldt, that you said you would like a tortoise for the garden? I remember exactly what you said, it was so witty.' (Caroline looks witty.) ' "You can buy a tortoise any hour of the day or night in the Corso Umberto in Naples. But in Harrods it's 'No' after the first of September." '

Out comes the hand with a tortoise! And there's another. One for each of us.

'Did I say that?' asks Caroline, taking her tortoise.

'One is the male and the other is the little female. (Tee-hee.) They are in good condition. In fact they were mating yesterday, when I bought them.'

'Oh, poor things. So public.'

'Not at all,' says the Persian, changing his tack at once. 'It was a very private garden. No one could see in. There was some moss and stones. Even I did not know what was happening until I heard this whistling noise.'

'What whistling noise?' We look suspiciously at our tortoises, which are silent.

Prostitutess picks up her pekinese in case one of the tortoises should start whistling at it. We all three pet our livestock silently.

'They whistle at one another, it's extraordinary. And then you hear this clapping.'

'Clapping? I didn't know tortoises could clap. Surely their hands don't meet?' When I say this Caroline looks at me quite sternly. But you must admit it's highly ridiculous.

'They clap their shells together, like this.' He joins the palms of his Persian hands. 'The male makes a tremendous effort, you know, standing up on his hind legs. And he pants, really Mrs Vandeveldt, the poor fellow gasps for breath. He strains with his neck' (the Persian stretches his neck out of his dark grey shirt) 'and, you know, you can see the muscle beating and beating in the flesh of his neck.'

This is really grim. Caroline *ought* to be looking at me under her eyelashes and laughing to me. But she *isn't*.

'I had no idea,' says Caroline. 'It's fascinating.'

'Marvellous,' says Prostitutess. 'I had always wondered.'

'One thing is certain,' I say, 'tortoises are *noisy*.'

At that moment, more rattling of wooden beads, and Killi's head and shoulders are with us. He's come straight from the sun, and although red in the face, has a head like a handsome bullet and is also broad-shouldered. He smiles benevolently; obviously must have managed to tint his legs.

Caroline lifts her tortoise up to him and says cheerfully:

'Boo! They whistle when they mate.'

A single glance tells Killi where the tortoises have come from. The Persian now seems to be holding his basket in a guilty fashion. He looks over-anxious to please and grins hopefully at Killi. His whole attitude is that of a beseeching, uneasy dog-like vendor of tortoises. Killi promptly sneezes, and withdraws his head.

'Darling!' calls Prostitutess helplessly, but it's too late.

We're left to pick up the pieces. Caroline does her best with the Persian. She plays with his basket, she feels how cool the grass is, she looks up at him with her English complexion, she practically whistles at him; but he is crushed and won't be comforted. Whatever his astrologer told him about the deal with Killi, it would take a strong man to carry it through now. My part of the homage from an Eastern man to a Western woman is on a low table where I put it, eating a green straw hat belonging to Prostitutess. What an emotion-packed morning!

6

Dyson has done it! All alone, with nothing but that Italian phrase-book and its inadequate gardening section ('How do the grafts get on?') he's cut down Purzelbaum's lemon tree by remote control. Beetle says he saw him in communion with one of the locals, a dim but jovial fellow. Dyson appeared to be interviewing him as though on English television, taking a great interest in him and in his family. Obviously this is the way to get your gardening done, because the man promised that not one flower-head should remain on its stalk. He understood all about hay fever; it turns out that one-third of the population of Italy suffers from hay fever, and children have to be made in the winter because the men spend the pollen months sneezing over their wives, who consequently reject them. I haven't noticed this. But still, they do tend to have paved gardens without flowerbeds as a national feature, so it may be true.

We haven't been near the scene of the crime. I hardly dare to think about it, remembering Purzelbaum's clairvoyance, in case he intercepts my thoughts and confronts me. I have a picture of the lemon tree in my head, just a dental stump with the leafy top and all its lemons lying in the dust.

We wait all afternoon for some explosion. I expect to see flames or at least steam shooting out of the mountain-side where Purzelbaum's house is. I go bathing with Beetle and the children, who are always giving one another questionnaires. They talk about student power and not being dowdy. They are closely in touch with the Persian, and report on his activities. Apparently he was last seen in conversation with the Mayor of Livone, and called him 'Caro Sindaco'. I'm sure Killi is making the mistake of a lifetime.

The following morning, I've just got my bathing costume on and I'm on the terrace with the tortoises, all three warming our backs in the sun, when Beetle appears.

'Darling, you've no idea!' He kisses and hugs me.

'Oh Beetle, *be quick*!'

'The garden was an absolute shambles, a wreck. We could see it from Rupert's balcony. I had to go indoors, it was so awful. And the lemon tree stump was so *white*. Nobody knows exactly when Purzelbaum came back and saw it. There was a terrible silence. Rupert, incidentally, didn't know a thing. Too busy with Mrs Voos ... Well, at five o'clock this morning' (Beetle is seething with merriment) 'there was a steady hammering noise, and I went out in my dressing-gown to see what was going on –'

'I can't wait! Purzelbaum?'

'There were some workmen in his garden, putting up a garage! They'd got the poles up – that was the hammering – and were just roofing the thing over. Now the point is, this garage is directly in front of Rupert's terrace, where he often has tea when he's alone and does his writing, and it cuts out his view of the sea.'

'Poor Rupert. How awful.'

'I was just taking it all in when Rupert himself came out and joined me, also in dressing-gown. He was simply electrified. He said it was a flagrant breach of faith between two old friends and neighbours. And he went straight out, just as he was, bedroom slippers and all, and walked down to Purzelbaum's to stop it. Of course when he got there, Purzelbaum was waiting for him and pointed silently to his garden. Rupert was in such despair about the garage he didn't realise the garden had been wrecked, he merely thought the workmen had been clearing the ground in order to get on with their diabolical garage, and he didn't pay any attention to the gesture. So Purzelbaum got even angrier and called out that Rupert's nettles were seeding onto his land.'

'Crikey!'

'Rupert was dumbfounded, and said as far as he knew he hadn't got any nettles.'

'Purzelbaum then said that since Rupert's whole garden was a solid mass of weeds, he wouldn't know the difference. They went on like this, and David and I were standing on the balcony watching these two figures below us and feeling ghastly about it. The only thing to do was to go down to Purzelbaum and own up.'

'Yes, of course. Beetle, how awful!'

'So David and I went down in our dressing-gowns – honestly you never saw so many mad Englishmen out at five in the morning in their dressing-gowns! – only to meet Rupert on the way back with eyes like chips of granite. And at that instant a car reversed furiously out of Purzelbaum's house, covering us all in dust, and drove off down the road. Then we all trailed back to Rupert's, and on the way we explained what had happened. And bit by bit it sank in that we were the criminals.'

'I should have stopped you.'

'You couldn't have done. It was the combined rage of three insulted men, and it had to come out.'

'How did Rupert take it?'

'He simmered down, as much as he could. He said the difficulty was that at base Purzelbaum was a kind-hearted man with a genuine compassion for real sickness. And that he had been known to apologise after one of his fits of bad behaviour.'

'Huh!'

'Rupert kept going out to look at the garage from his terrace, and saying he didn't know what on earth he was going to do, because once a thing is up it's so difficult to get it down again.'

'But, Beetle, what made Purzelbaum think it was Rupert in the first place?'

'Rupert says Purzelbaum has always thought he, Rupert, was jealous of his garden. And he's been looking for a grievance anyway ever since Rupert got his knighthood. He remembers hearing about those nettles soon afterwards, but they vanished for several years. He says he thinks Purzelbaum felt *he* was somehow knighted at the same time, although it wasn't made public, and that he's been mentally playing at being Sir Oskar Purzelbaum ever since.'

'Well, that's not too bad, considering what some people play at mentally!'

'Yes, darling. I know you're my wicked dove.'

'Am I, Beetle?'

'Of course you are. You don't think these things would happen if you weren't here, do you?'

'*And* Caroline.'

'Yes, she helps. But it's chiefly you. Anyway, Caroline's busy fighting for her personality at the moment.'

'It doesn't say much for marriage, does it?' I look at him steadily. 'I think the whole thing's a myth. Caroline says she dreads the week-ends in England.'

'You can have a jolly marriage,' says Beetle, sitting down and taking my hand. 'In fact you've *got* to have a jolly one these days to keep off the cancer and migraine.' He laughs at himself. And then pulls a long face to match mine.

'It's got to be a natural jolliness,' I say.

'Of course it has. No cancer's going to be fooled by false jolliness.'

'My ideal of happiness is reading in bed.'

'Oh well then, you're going to be very easy to satisfy.'

'Caroline says she has claustrophobic dreams that she's bricked in and the last little gap of light is being filled in down in the far corner. And she wakes up with her fingers under the chest of drawers, trying desperately to lift it up.'

'That shows she has a very strong grip on life.'

'Beetle, you don't care!'

'Oh yes I do. I know perfectly well what Caroline is going through. Their marriage has got to grow up.'

'And ours hasn't even begun! God, I feel weak.'

'I'll strengthen you.' Beetle puts his arm around me and then takes it away. Here are Killi and the children. They've been down to the village to get bread and mortadello for lunch. Rety and Dyson are with them, so everyone's heard the story of this morning's five o'clock garage. We re-discuss it, trying to get the garage smaller as we do so. Rety calls it 'instant garage'. Killi says men must be found and paid to reduce the height of the poles; he says Rupert would be wise to consult a lawyer and also the Mayor of Livone. James suddenly comes out in his clear voice with:

'We can ask Mr Chamoun to help. He knows the Mayor. They call each other "darling".'

'Who's Mr Chamoun?' asks Killi. He's naked but for a pair of navy-blue Bermuda shorts (no English pantaloons for Killi) and a bitter lemon with a single lump of ice in it which jingles like a frosted sleigh-bell against the sides of the glass.

'Mummy's Persian. He's fabulous. He rings up Zurich from the local barber's shop while they're shaving him every morning. He has friction and neck massage. We know because we traced him there.'

'*Chamoun,*' says Killi miserably. 'It couldn't be Abu'l Akbar Chamoun?'

'Yes, Daddy, of course. Mr A. A. Chamoun. I've seen his Diners' Club card.'

Oh what a disintegration! I've never seen anything like it. Killi's face seems to fall in as though it's been mined in the middle. His tummy sticks out abruptly over the shorts, which shrink and in seconds look ridiculous on such a bulky man. His ice-bell tinkles in his hand with a faithless summer music. I can't help looking up in case the sun has gone in too; it's still there, but weaker.

I want to laugh at him, but I can't. Setbacks are incredibly serious to a man like Killi. After years of contact-making,

Killi knows everyone there is to know in the banking, insurance, and investment world. In fact he thinks that *is* the world. And there are days when I begin to think so too. But just at this moment Killi has fallen through a hole in his world and with a thump is down in the natural world with us. For example, the children are pushing lettuce leaves at the tortoises which stride forward, ignoring them, like ugly sisters trampling down gift wrappings. Killi just about rates as equal interest-value, but only just. He stirs in his wretchedness and tries to interest himself in what's going on. Suddenly he bends down and makes an overture to one of the tortoises by brushing his fingers under its chin. Tortoise promptly ducks its head in and looks out at him with seedy wisdom. 'Mind your fingers, Sonny Jim!'

'I thought they liked that,' says Killi without hope. Being rejected by a tortoise is just an additional blow.

'The thing is not to dislocate their necks,' I say with friendly malice. I know perfectly well why he's petting them; they're Chamoun's tortoises.

'We ought to build a proper enclosure for them, with a cave and wire netting,' says Killi. 'They can't wander around like this. One of the dogs might eat them.'

'They've been perfectly all right for nearly twenty-four hours.'

'In the meantime, we must get a large cool container, a hutch or a basket, and ... line it with fresh grass!' says Killi, getting better with every second. 'James, which barber's shop does Mr Chamoun go to?'

'The one in the piazza, by Leonardo's bar. They've got white telephones.'

Killi, whose metabolism is psychosomatically linked to

his business interests, seems to need a shave. He touches his chin; definitely rough.

'I might look in there.'

'Would you like the phrase-book?' asks Dyson. 'It really is invaluable.' He shoots off to get it.

On the whole sympathy is with Killi because his despair is so great and his plans to overcome it are so obvious and clumsy. It's the sheer effort he puts up which is touching and makes you respect him.

'It's extremely funny,' says Dyson coming back and looking up 'With the hairdresser'. 'And don't think for a moment these antiquated phrases are out of date. They work like a charm. The main thing is to put your heart and soul into it, because they take everything very seriously here.' (He thinks he's on the moon.)

'Certainly,' says Killi, who has never been more serious. 'And quite right too.'

'You could read bits out to Chamoun,' I say, looking over Dyson's shoulder. 'Honestly, Killi, this hairdresser piece is a work of genius. Shall we read it over to you?'

'Yes, if it doesn't take too long.' He looks at his watch, back on form. The Chamoun hunt is on!

'It starts off:

'"Ah! You have put the brush into my mouth."'

'"It was because you spoke when I did not expect it. The young bride's hair was blank, thick, coarse, her forehead broad and square. (Just the thing for Chamoun.) An ordinary hairdresser would not have been able to hide the sternness of her features; but I have given her head a gentle and languishing expression."'

'"Truly, I am struck with admiration,"' reads Dyson.

'"But, mister artist, with all your talent you have cut me; I am bleeding. You have been shaving against the grain."'

'"No, sir; I have only taken off a little pimple (*una bollicella*, Killi). With a bit of court-plaster, it will not be seen."'

'"Are not my moustaches too long?"' asks Dyson anxiously. '"And my whiskers?"'

'"They sit well round your face, sir."'

'"Don't my hair require to be freshened up a little?"'

'"I will cut a little off behind; but I would not touch the tuft on the forehead nor about the ears,"' I read, looking up at Killi and trying not to laugh. (He's deadly serious; listening intently!)

'"Why not?"'

'"Because, sir, you would then appear to have too low a forehead and ears too long. Do you wish me to give you a touch of the curling irons, sir?"'

'"It is unnecessary; my hair curls naturally,"' says Dyson vigorously.

'"Shall I put on a little oil or pomatum?"'

'"Put on a little scented oil."'

'"Please to look in the glass."'

'"It will do very well. I see you are an artist worthy to shave and trim your contemporaries,"' Dyson finishes with style.

'There, Killi! All good, useful stuff. That's what life is all about.' I hand him the book. 'But you won't start sneezing, will you? Because there's no dialogue for that.'

'There will be soon,' says Beetle, 'once the word gets out about Purzelbaum's garden. We'll be getting phrase-books full of completely useless dialogues, starting: "Did you cut down my lemon tree this morning?"'

'Afternoon,' says Dyson.

'Or; "When did you last see your tortoises?"' I say.

'Think what they'll do with the thermal baths! "We must drain the baths because the Germans are kissing!" No wonder people in England find it difficult to "think" in other languages. It never occurs to them that these phrases are taken straight from life. And up to date life at that,' says Rety.

Killi listens to us all. Once again, although smiling, he manages to look martyred and superior.

'I only wish I could stay and enjoy it with you,' he says, sighing and turning off down the path. He is completely happy, with all his financial burdens back in place. He goes off, leaving us with the feeling that he's earning all our livings. Somehow I don't think that phrase-book will do him much good with Chamoun though; different sense of humour. It could make things even worse than they are already. We still don't know who Chamoun is, but one thing is definite: he's incredibly wealthy and influential.

Waterloo Barns has a library in the via Roma, just before you go into the piazza. The outside wall is like all Italian walls, stone with lumps gouged out and a patina of pure grey grime. Waterloo's dirt is sacred, bookish dirt. There are old, bound volumes in the narrow window, and brand-new despatch cases in plastic, especially constructed for carrying books. I covet one of these, especially the frog-green one, which looks like a bit of a Rolls-Royce, shiny and having buckles. I fancy carrying a frog-green lecture in it.

Inside, Waterloo can be seen in the international bookman's posture: slumped over a corner table with a lamp and a record-player, giving yellow light and old yellow piano music. There's nearly always someone sitting on the other side of the table, discussing their problems. Today Caroline and myself are there, and believe me, we've got plenty to discuss.

Waterloo is the nicest sort of American. He has fair tufted hair and gives an impression of worn youthfulness. He's probably forty-seven. Most people on the island are. His great quality in his interest in every aspect of life; his liking for gossip equals his liking for dates and facts in Italian history and culture. Also he gives you a sense of your own life (no wonder you feel grateful to him) by drawing comparisons with other lives from his wide reading. He adds to your reality with what was once the reality of others.

And he *didn't* go to Purzelbaum's baths, in spite of Prostitutess. He says he hasn't been parted from his clothes for a good ten years, and, like his empty bed for one person, he thinks it's become a habit. He says Purzelbaum insults him regularly once a week, but that he is essentially a good man, in fact indispensable to the island.

'And he was very, very interested,' says Waterloo, 'when Rupert cut down his tree.'

'*Interested?*'

'Very. You see, he was half expecting it.'

'Not clairvoyant again!'

'Oh no. This is pure medical deduction. He says Rupert has been showing signs of a middle-aged sex neurosis.'

'Oh ha-ha. Who hasn't?' says Caroline carelessly.

'It's a serious matter.' Waterloo rolls himself a cigarette from an old tin box of tobacco.

'So Rupert cuts down trees? Which he didn't anyway.'

'The Doctor is afraid Rupert is now impotent.' Waterloo brings it out like a piece of pompous dogma. Heavens, he's taking it for granted, and is upset when we both burst out laughing together.

'Waterloo, you are such a duck! Are you telling us that Dr Purzelbaum thinks Rupert cut down his tree because he can't –?' Dare I use the word 'erection' in front of Waterloo? I think not.

Waterloo nods decisively. He says:

'These things are vital in the composition of certain men. The Doctor says he has known of cases where a middle-aged male, a member of a large family, cut down a whole *avenue* of trees because his relations would not come and stay with him in the country.'

More laughter. Waterloo has so much sex knowledge and takes it so seriously, his innocence is positively indecent.

'He ought to be pleased,' says Caroline. 'I'm simply delighted when people *don't* come and stay with me. I'd even plant trees to keep them away.'

'Stop!' I wave at her. 'I'm getting dizzy. Trees up, trees down, there's no peace here. And it's supposed to be a holiday.'

'I wonder if we ought to tell Rupert he's impotent?' Caroline is joking.

'Oh surely, don't people know?'

'Not if they haven't tested themselves recently with the real thing.'

'What about Pros – Madeleine Voos?'

'Charming Mrs Voos,' says Waterloo very warmly. 'The Doctor says she is the root cause of all the trouble. The Doctor says that if Rupert takes the cure down at the baths, he can take care of all his problems with Mrs Voos.'

'But we're talking as though it's true! Whereas Rupert hasn't *got* any problems! He's a healthy, happy man in full functioning order.' Caroline adds, 'And he wouldn't dream of cutting down anyone's trees, even if he was stone-cold impotent.'

'You'll never get the Doctor to believe that, I'm afraid.' Waterloo is still entirely sober on the subject. 'He tells me that people cut down trees when they don't get enough love in their lives, and don't feel wanted. The next step is suicide.'

I can see from the look on Caroline's face that she's going to put him right once and for all about Rupert and the tree. I'm afraid her language may be rough.

'Old buggerluggs Vespasian doesn't know that Ronald Dyson cut down his footling tree, Waterloo, and it's your duty to tell him. As for Rupert, his whole life is jam-crammed to the eye-teeth with sex and love and being wanted.'

'And this is no moment, Waterloo, to put the word around that he's impotent.' Myself, very strong.

'If it gets to his ears,' says Caroline with dark blue in her eyes, 'it might actually *make* him impotent. Too mean. Some men are so sensitive that, when they go off for their adultery, the mere sight of a sign with "Buckingham Hotel" written on it is quite enough to make them impotent on the spot. They call it "strange hotel impotence".'

Waterloo has caught our infection (at last!), and is smiling.

'I give you my word of honour not to put the news about. And I certainly will tell the Doctor exactly what happened. Though I'm afraid I'll get it in the neck.'

'Don't do that. Please. We'll have to worry about you.'

'Waterloo, is it safe for you,' – I'm concerned about him – 'sitting here, vulnerable to anyone who comes in?'

'I'm a peaceful man.'

'But you get battered.'

'It keeps me alive. I like people.'

'But you're always mopping up spilt lives. It's awful.'

'I have my salon here. No, I'm fine.' He gets up, disturbed at being pitied.

'Well, in that case' – I suddenly feel practical – 'let's get down to the question of that garage. It's *got* to be lowered. Rupert's whole life revolves around his Lapsang-Typhoo tips on the terrace.'

'Oh God, wasn't it awful!' Caroline laughs.

'If Purzelbaum doesn't bring that garage down and stop getting at poor, harmless Rupert, I can't answer for the consequences. You've seen our three extra men?'

'Yes,' says Waterloo doubtfully.

'Well then! They're capable of anything, I can tell you. Rety has the mad ideas, Dyson is the con man, and Beetle is ...' I think for a long time rejecting one word after another. In the end I mutter to myself, 'So sweet.'

'And Killi,' says Caroline, with her claws out, looking sharply at me.

'And Killi, who can literally fix *anything*, if he wants to, and is tall, dark, handsome, bad-tempered and kind.' I look straight back at Caroline. She nods gloomily. 'Where is he today, Caroline?'

'He's out looking for Chamoun again. We had to spend five thousand lire on a silly old basket for the tortoises! Sickening! He carries them about with him. Honestly, if we didn't have the children's travel allowances we'd be broke.'

'Chamoun?' says Waterloo helpfully. 'He was in here only this morning. A very cultivated man. We've had many good conversations.'

'The white-haired one is playing up,' says Caroline. 'Poor Killi's in and out of that barber's shop a hundred times a day. He's been clipped, shampooed, manicured, pedicured, massaged and frictioned. Not to mention being talked at. There's hardly a hair left on him, and he stinks to heaven!'

'You don't suppose he's got the wrong barber?'

'That's what Killi thought, so we had to go into all the others and buy bottles of completely useless eau-de-cologne. It really hurt.'

'What about the beach?'

'The children are covering that. James has binoculars, so if Chamoun were even to swim around the point, right out to sea, James would spot him. Ossie and Tim have been down to the baths, checking up on the mud and massage.'

'And to think that only three days ago you couldn't put your nose out of doors without running into him!'

'Couldn't even have breakfast!'

'Describing his habits to everyone! Publicly.'

'Anybody's dog for a bone.'

'Caroline means that she was thinking of taking him as a l – –'

Caroline, well up in the polite karate of an English boarding school, borrows one of its inbred movements from her past. She gets the muscle of my thigh, just above the knee, between her thumb and fingers, and gives it a quick pinch. 'I *wasn't*.'

'Horseplay,' says Waterloo, suddenly guarding his record-player. He decides to calm us down; after all, there are expensive records about. And some of these books have slips of tissue paper marking essential information ten or twenty years old. They flutter. Whoa!

'Perhaps I can bring them together,' he says.

'First find your Chamois!' I'm nearly out of control.

'Feed it on biscuits,' says Caroline.

'Give it a hot thermal bath.'

'*Cherchez la* forty-three-year-old *femme.*'

'Devalue the franc.'

'And the consequence is a tortoise.'

'All right!' says Waterloo, 'do you *want* me to help?'

'Oh yes please, Waterloo. We do really. It's just the strain that makes us behave like this.'

'Well, perhaps I can find a common interest between them . . .'

'Money,' says Caroline thoughtlessly.

'Something more . . . spiritual. Maybe of a literary nature?'

We both shudder. Caroline racks her brain. Finally she says:

'Killi wrote a thick pamphlet called "Partnership Law and Financial Suicide in 1967". He's terribly proud of it, and always has a few copies with him. He's also written something for the Masons.'

'You mean he's a Mason too?' Waterloo is excited.

'Yes, if he's paid his fees.'

'Oh well then, our trouble is nearly over, because so is Mr Chamoun.'

'Everybody is these days. It's like flying Lufthansa, everyone's done it. You get a tin badge and things to wear.'

'Aprons.' This is an obvious remark coming from me, but I can never resist it and I don't see why I should. I don't have to prove things all the time.

'If Killi brought me a copy of his pamphlet, *signed* and dedicated reverently to Mr Chamoun, christian names here, and I indicated to Mr Chamoun that Killi was about to leave the island, or had already left . . . and that he was a brother Mason . . . and that he was really in low spirits about the mix-up . . .'

'Chamoun might feel inclined to speak to Killi again?'

'If he bumped into him by chance.'

'What about Chamoun's love for Caroline?' I ask them both.

'I think it's all part of businessman's love-making,' says Caroline. 'If he's financially in love with Killi, it brushes off on me. They go beyond the point of real feelings. They're anaesthetised in the balls (sorry, Waterloo) if it's anything to do with business. That's why they have to sleep with belly dancers. Because they know what they feel with them.'

'What about their wives?'

'They're stooges. They end up growing grey moustaches. You've seen all those expensive adverts for unwanted hair? Well then.'

'How's yours, Carol?'

'Coming on nice and thick. I can comb it with my mascara brush.'

'Let me have the pamphlet,' says Waterloo, 'and then keep Killi at home all day. Mr Chamoun is not a vindictive man. He needs something for his pride though –'

'They don't normally have too much of that,' says Caroline. 'Not if it goes against their interests.'

I must say, Waterloo has been a tower of strength. We leave him, feeling much better. I even have the impression that some of the books lying around us while he talked have been read *right through*; amazing.

Outside we run straight into Killi and the children. James has an Italian newspaper reporting on the Paris situation. We read: *'La Crisi Galoppa!'* Killi says:

'He was quite right about them whistling. One of them started up a few minutes ago, when I was sitting in the piazza. It's quite extraordinary.' He looks down complacently at his basket as though he's achieved something.

'Tootled a few notes? Or all on the same one?' I ask.

'Sort of high-pitched.'

'Sounds like Purzelbaum's hearing aid. It *is* sexy, now you mention it.'

'At least they're not impotent,' says Caroline. 'Darling, what is Chamoun? Is he a gnome?'

'He's about six gnomes rolled into one. I've been wanting to meet him for years, but we always seem to miss. He's elusive. He's on all sides at once and his own side. Sort of Kim Philby of the money world.'

'He doesn't sound very trustworthy.'

'That's where you're wrong. He is. When you're dealing in thousands of pounds, you've simply got to trust people or you'd never do a deal. There's an almost fool-hardy trust necessary to do deals with near-strangers in big finance. Whereas on the lower levels, in ordinary business, nobody trusts anybody.' He's happy to be able to talk on his subject, and kisses Caroline gratefully for it.

We tell him that Waterloo Barns is going to help.

7

'Beetle, I must stop crying every morning. It's a waste of time.'

'I know. Unhappy people waste an awful lot of time.'

'It's just that I feel it's my duty to her – to think about her. And every morning I wake up with a fresh insight into her life. Beetle, it was such an enchanting, gay little life, and now she's lost it – it's just run out of her as if out of a bottle. And I've lost it forever.'

'Yes, well, you're giving out the same sort of irreplaceable pleasure to other people in your turn. Me, for example.'

'I didn't appreciate her.'

'Yes, you did.'

'I keep going back and trying to put things right for her. As though she was still alive!'

'People don't want to go on living forever, you know. They die when they come to the end of their ideas.'

'Beetle, if *you* die it'll be the absolute end.'

He comes close and carefully puts a number of wet kisses along my temples. We're standing up on a mule path cut into the mountainside. It sounds boring, but it isn't. Under our feet the solid gleaming bluestone goes up almost vertically. When it gets too vertical, there are peasant steps cut in it. It's wise to hurry on through these narrow bits, in case you meet a mule head on. And they carry barrels, in addition. I imagine meeting a mule, flattening myself against the rock, being nibbled by yellow teeth with lips pulled back from them, and then kicked by an iron hoof as it passes. But chiefly being buffeted by its head. They're big too. The only reason I've stopped walking is that my grief is greater than my fear.

We go on and come out every few yards on a new terrace and vineyards. In spite of the size of the mules (I forgot to mention, these mules puff loudly and make their lips vibrate), everything else is small. Small cuts of land are propped up on stones. There are brand-new, coloured wild flowers, a pleasant buzzing and murmuring, very good green weeds filled with drops of water, and so many butterflies it's a bit bogus. It's like a pantomime stage, with the same warm brightly-lit air. I frown and say:

'I'm not sure she wasn't indispensable to my happiness.'

'Rubbish.'

'Well, I was indispensable to hers, and I didn't give her my physical presence.'

'People can't expect too much from relationships across the generation gap. They must build on friendships with their own generation.'

'You can't if you don't find the right kind of people.'

'Well, it's no good making children because you can't find the right kind of friends in life, and trying to bring up little friends for yourself.'

I stop again, and shake my head to try to throw out the painful thoughts.

'I suppose I must carry on her work.'

'What work was that, darling?'

'The work of making the world more delightful and reassuring so that people would want to live in it.'

Beetle never makes fun of innocent, meagre philosophy. He knows I am making an effort to throw off my grief so that I can use the past instead of being hurt by it.

There are tears that suddenly smart on the eyeballs, as though they strike from outside like sleet, they are so salt and hard and burning hot.

'Oh Beetle, I didn't go to her when she wanted me! At that particular moment, I didn't have enough happiness over in my life to give to her. And I underestimated the gravity of things. I'm that sort of person, Beetle. Without a proper sense of the responsibilities of life. I forgot that people's bodies get frail. I just don't think I'll ever get over this death.' And I do, in fact, feel that it will engulf me. 'How can I live with it?'

He puts his pale English arms around me and makes that comforting circle which is like the hearth of a warm fire. My burst of crying is short; I'm buried in his aertex shirt and can't get air. I try to be neat about it, but crying, real crying, is primitive like vomiting. I stop and say half-angrily:

'If only she hadn't enjoyed things quite so much – a good film, or an opera, or a book. It's too bad of her! And then they go and bury her so deeply in the ground, at least seven feet down, so far away from life!' I can see the grave-yard and the false bright green turf they use to camouflage the raw earth of a newly dug grave. 'Beetle, the service was the most materialistic thing I've ever heard. Canon Walters kept harping on how *young* she looked for her age, and how astonished he was to find out she was sixty-three. All he could find words for was for his astonishment. He was totally incapable of comprehending the sort of person he was burying. I mentally apologised to my mother for having allowed someone of religious feeling so inferior to her own to bury her.'

'Most people care a great deal about the way they look. Didn't she?' asks Beetle intelligently.

'Oh yes!' He's clever, because of course she was just as good a materialist as the noxious priest. 'My appearance, her appearance, everybody's appearance. She was down on it like a ton of bricks. We all had to have good faces, good posture and so on. Honestly Beetle, I get absolutely fed up with this phrase "good-looking". There are times when you just can't be good-looking, you're in too much of a hurry, too interested in ideas. And in English-German circles it's the criterion for a whole estimate of character.'

'And in Italian?'

'Oh!' I smile with pleasure at the thought of Italian society. 'In Italian circles, high, low and medium, there's somebody for everybody. And looks are all relative.'

We're already walking on, holding hands. I begin to see what kind of a man Beetle is, in guiding me away from my misery towards safe, idle generalities. I press his hand to indicate my appreciation, and out of gratitude fix my chatter on the future.

'Suppose we run into Chamoun? He's not down there,' pointing to the village far below (a dog barks from it) and the beaches curving away around the island, 'so he's probably up here. I do hope he gives Killi a second chance.'

'Oh everyone gets second, and third, chances in life, that's the nice thing about it.'

'Except in the case of a death,' say my thoughts, but I'm silent.

'We don't know things are going to happen when they do, darling, otherwise we'd behave differently.' Beetle packs up my death thoughts with this solid sentence. But still he waits patiently, not abruptly changing the subject, in case I want to go on. No! I think I'll take ten minutes of life while my conscience isn't looking.

'Beet!' I call out in flighty cocktail intonation. 'Could you remember something for me?'

'Might.'

I look at him. His head is sunny and thoughtless now. We seem to be entering the swooning, classical *dolce far niente* part of the afternoon, an envelope of heat-haze and glances that soften bones.

'You've already forgotten it before I've told it to you!'

'Yes!'

'I say, Sawdust! Test my eyesight by asking me what things are.'

'What's that brown lump ahead of us?'

'A rock.'

'No, it's a mule.'

'Beetle!' My heart bangs itself wastefully.

'Suppose you had a mule farm, and had to milk them every day!'

'Funny. I thought you were forty years old.'

'All right then, I'll test your ears.'

'No, don't. They're dirty.'

'I know they are. They've got bitter stuff in them. I always thought I was the only one who had bitter stuff in my ears. I was very relieved when I found you had it too.'

'This conversation isn't about anything.'

'I think I ought to make love to you up here.'

'Ought you?'

Damn. We've got ourselves into a nice private vineyard and there's a man in it. One might as well be in Piccadilly Circus.

He comes towards us. He's got a gun and a dog, and coming to us down the angle of the mountain through the amber air, puts all three of us in the incomparable film of 'The Leopard'. Or am I sitting in the Odeon Cinema in Haverstock Hill, watching it? And there'll be a winter night outside, and sleet on the steps of the cinema. And everyone will hurry out, dragging on brown coats, looking frowsty and hoping like hell they don't meet anyone they know. And for a good fifteen minutes I'll be accident-prone, with a head full of magic, unable to walk slowly or be polite to anyone. Good old days!

No, this time I'm *in it,* and completely at home. He makes us welcome, it's his vineyard but he knows my Aunt Evie and wants us to take some lemons. He picks four big ones. Beetle carries them away. We beam and smile and paw the ground like a couple of Purzelbaum's German stallions. God, it's repulsive. That reminds me, I never checked up on Beetle's reaction to the actual hot water thing. I say:

'Beetle, did you enjoy the thermal baths?'

He's not alerted to the fact that this is one of my tests for right-thinking masculinity, and answers:

'Yes.'

'*Did* you?'

'The bit I had, yes. Didn't get much.'

'You didn't feel enervated, flaccid, vaguely like Caligula, queer, decadent, like potted crab meat?'

'No. And I didn't feel like Catullus either.'

'Oh. You enjoyed it?'

'Well, actually for the first time in my life I realised that this was always what I'd imagined swimming should be like. Warm.'

'Are you English?'

'This is a perfectly normal English reaction.'

'You ought to have got out straight away instead of letting your skin go soggy.'

'It didn't have time to go soggy.'

'How long would you have spent in if you'd been left in peace?'

'Probably all the morning.'

'God. This is awful. You've given yourself away.'

'Oh good.'

'You can't imagine George Orwell in that filthy hot water, can you?'

'Yes, of course. I can just see him swimming up and down with Lampedusa. "Swim, George, swim. Show them your son swimmer. Swim like the snow-white swans swam, you know how the snow-white swans swam, George."' Beetle actually goes so far as to hum the tune to this old piece of drivel. '"Six sharp shivering sharks are nibbling at your limbs, so a swim well swum is a swum well swim. Swim, George, swim, George, SWIM!"' He ends up singing loudly.

Some people pass us along the path, and I hiss at him:

'The lemons!'

Beetle immediately gives the impression of having stolen them. He looks over his shoulder guiltily.

'Quick. Wrap them in your lemon-coloured handkerchief. We can't come out of the vineyards singing and carrying lemons.'

Beetle goes into the pocket of his trousers reluctantly. He doesn't want me to know he's still living off the same handkerchief.

I encourage him by saying:

'It's all right! I've seen Dyson's underwear. And I'm still alive.'

Beetle stops and says:

'Now I've got a perfectly clear conscience about these lemons . . .'

'All the evidence is against you.'

'It's worse still to come out carrying a bundle, as though you're covering something up.'

'They can only speculate then. Whereas now they can *see*.'

'All right. Just to please you.'

He brings out the famous handkerchief. It's rank. Does it offset the thermal baths blunder? I'll have to ask Prostitutess. We make knots in it, and it looks like a fantastically dirty pair of underpants with somebody still inside them.

'I can't' – he laughs, and it's the laughter of weakness – 'carry *that*.'

'I'll carry it for you then.'

'No!' He snatches it back quickly. 'Can't we leave the lemons here? After all, we don't want them.'

'*Sacred* lemons?'

After a while, he says mournfully:

'I know. It's because I enjoyed the thermal baths. I *thought* something was wrong.'

'I'm a brute, a martinet, a kill-joy, a huzzy, just a female Purzelbaum. *Please* forgive me.'

It was established; we were in love.

Meanwhile, back at the villa . . .

Oh! Oh! Oh! The *festa,* I'd forgotten all about it. We're all going, of course. Caroline and Killi are dining out somewhere together; I'll go with Beetle, and I expect Dyson and Rety will tag along. They've been sticking like glue so far; they seem afraid to go out on their own, like maiden ladies. Dyson sneaks off up to Rupert's to play poker with David Rety in the evening. Can you imagine it! An Italian night, with a violet velvet landscape, not too hot at all on account of the mountain dew that falls so suddenly at ten o'clock you could drink it; your eyes soon get accustomed to the darkness, and you can go off anywhere. There's the piazza to gossip in, with two set times for different brands of people: six o'clock, all humanity that earns its living, eats regular meals and obeys time; eight o'clock onward, the night-birds, intelligentsia and other ruffians. Then there are the restaurants, smart and native, the night-clubs (two), not to mention goings-on around the ping-pong table at the thermal baths, private parties, and all the witchcraft of a long spice-scented walk in the refreshing darkness. Poker! And they read English newspapers which they crackle all the time as if they're doing up Christmas parcels. Dyson loves that noise. When I asked them why they didn't go out in the evenings, Dyson said there was no electric light and the roads weren't made up, so he was afraid of twisting his ankle. I said he could have my torch and the seicento (belonging to Aunt Evie). And one evening they actually went off together and played ping-pong; the only trouble was that the moment came when Dyson realised he wasn't losing by accident! So they came back early, hardly speaking to one another, and Beetle and I were foiled again. So far this is the most frustrating holiday I've ever had. Dyson is improving, though. Ever since his gardening success he's stopped singing *The Donkey Serenade* (perhaps he tried to sing it in the thermal baths and Purzelbaum simply couldn't stand it? After all, something concrete must have touched off that incident) and he's cut himself down to one short sharp kahk. We've cured him of saying 'loo' by doing a pantomime on the phrase *'garde à l'eau'*, during which Caroline made the motions of throwing a heavy chamberpot over Beetle, who ducked smartly. Since then Dyson hasn't been to it nearly so often and seems to be getting everything into better perspective. And when we ran out of tea the other day, he actually went and bought *teabags*, with his own money! It was a shock. He now makes, and drinks, most of the tea for Rupert. We have to shade our eyes as we walk by that terrible garage, it seems to give out malevolent purple shadows. Killi has been to the Mayor, but he is, literally, dough in Purzelbaum's hands. Purzelbaum is in the middle of making him a new dental plate, and you know what that means. The Mayor says his last set of teeth were as large as tombstones and he was afraid of chipping his already existing teeth with them if he enjoyed his food or got into an argument. He's as happy as a baby about getting new ones, and couldn't care less if the garage was a skyscraper. So Killi went to a lawyer who said that Purzelbaum had cured him of varicose veins, and as his ankles used to swell up and he went in deadly fear of losing the use of his legs, he didn't think there were adequate grounds for litigation in the matter of a temporary construction of wood and wattle which might easily be blown down anyway in the first storm (hint). And poor Killi has his own troubles, because he's developed backache since Chamoun has refused to see him. He always gets backache when he can't get his own way; he takes it out on Caroline, as it were, by taking it out on himself. Caroline says to me, 'I know what it's like, Mimi, because when he accelerates in the car it gives me a dull pain under my shoulder-blades, as though an undigested mutton chop was lying there.'

Killi lies down, groaning, on a towel on the terrace, and Caroline presses his back while he studies the tortoises as if they were made of solid platinum. There's not a thing he doesn't know about their habits and sex-life, talks of nothing else, and bores everyone to death. As Killi is an exceedingly clever man and as quick as a flash, this is a frightful situation. One thing is certain about that back of his, we'll have to cart him off to Purzelbaum unless Chamoun turns up. We've told Waterloo Barns about Killi's back, so that he can rub it in. He says he saw Chamoun and told him, but he didn't turn a hair. On the other hand, he was interested in Killi's literature, and took it off to read and vanished again. The hotel just says he's 'out'. The children practise giving one another Masonic handshakes; these vary from having a slug all ready in your hand to a full-sized effort to throw the brother Mason over your shoulder. They certainly never meet now without shaking one another by the hand. They also play a version of Happy Families which they improvised from a general knowledge test in *Queen*: 'Have you got Danny La Rue and Lester Piggott?' 'No. But I have got Julie Christie and Tito Gobbi.' They no longer have access to the hot line to Paris, so Caroline is feeling much easier in her mind. It's one thing having an effigy of Cohn-Bendit in sand on the beach, and quite another cooking pasta for him twice a day while he makes bombs in the kitchen.

By now Purzelbaum knows perfectly well who was responsible for his garden, and Dyson, Rety, and Beetle are very content to be known as the guilty ones. They still think it's inferior in insult value to being kept waiting in bathing trunks. Even now Rety chews it over: 'We ought to have tweaked his nose, as well.'

'You could have threatened it verbally,' says Beetle.

Rety tries it out:

'I'll pull your bloody nose!'

He waits for inspiration, while answering himself sardonically in the character of Purzelbaum: 'I'll pull *your* bloody nose.'

Dyson suddenly says:

'I'll pull your bloody clapped-up nose!' He looks at us hopefully.

Not bad! He really is coming on. He then asks in a very childlike manner:

'By the way, what is a *dablusci*?'

'WC,' says Beetle.

So that's it! Of course, I knew all the time, I simply

wasn't applying myself. Beetle is very good at international things.

'You know what we haven't done?' says Rety, still carrying on a running-fight with the Doctor.

'What?'

'Phoned him up. All that hoo-ha about "you can tell whether someone has a sexual problem by the way they answer the phone".'

'We'll do it tonight. After the *festa*. He won't be expecting it. It's perfect timing.'

'What shall we say?'

'Wait for the inspiration of the moment. Ronald can do it. His inspiration is extraordinary today.'

'No, thank you – I did the garden.'

'All right then, I'll do it,' says Rety. He was going to anyway, but Dyson has been such a new man since his gardening that he didn't want to deprive him of another opportunity for self-improvement.

At half past five when we're just about to leave, James comes hurtling back to the house with some good news.

Chamoun has responded! The old white-haired arch-manipulator and four-biscuit man has responded! Not in person exactly. But he's left with Waterloo Barns some literature of his own. A Rank Xerox of a handwritten report called (James has written it down) 'A Survey of Australian Stock, with Indications of Unit Trust Growth Limitations'. It's waiting for Killi in the library. James wasn't allowed to handle it. But it's there all right. Killi looks as though he's Moses suddenly being given the tablets of law. His terrible nagging backache, his groaning and apathy vanish as though they have never been. He springs up, nearly squashing the tortoises to a jelly in his eagerness to get at this vital manuscript. He nods to himself. Do I hear him say to Chamoun, 'I know your work of course'? He goes into his bedroom and changes his shirt. He comes out with a box of Havana cigars, and new shoes which are stiff and shimmer on his feet and make a loud noise crossing the marble floor. He looks magnificent, classical beefcake, and just about to charge. I suddenly remember two key phrases of Killi's which Caroline told to me. One: 'Businessmen have to be one dream ahead of each other.' And two: 'You've got to whack them over the head with a penis!'

'*Che bello uomo!*' says Caroline, appreciatively, kissing him. 'And so masculine. He even loves masculine parts of the world like Australia.'

We follow them outside into the silent garden as the sun goes down.

I'm dressed in yellow velvet bell-bottomed trousers, and I've got a matching short flowered velvet coat over them, tightly knotted in at the waist. It's got a plunge neckline, so I walk carefully like a model, with shoulders slightly rounded and stomach forward. I've wound an old Venetian glass necklace around my wrist in order to make an outsize, heavy, glassy bracelet. I already have to lift my trousers as I go, like a skirt, because the bushes of herbs along the path are still wet underneath with last night's dew. Fire-flies will be rising up shortly. I've got so much scent plastered on, up into my hair, behind my ears, under my chin, my whole head is temporarily embalmed, and I daren't move it much in case I let too much fresh air into the warm vapour. I spent twenty minutes getting my hair right up on the back of my head. Luckily my neck's brown, as are the hands I'm hanging loosely in my pockets, cool as sections of cucumber. I feel gentle and modest.

Beetle escorts me, loving it. Rety and Dyson are cowed by my sudden sophistication and follow up, arguing about Rupert's impotence in whispers. I can hear the whispering cross-talk behind me. La Prostitutess has heard of the smear and is furious. It's the most terrible insult, and she takes it very much to heart. In return, she has told everyone that Rupert is like a raging bull and wears her out. In the piazza, when she takes her Cinzano at 6.15 in the evening, she puts her feet up to rest herself, and she takes a micro-taxi to the beach every morning. She no longer leans forward when she talks, and she wears some very pretty cotton flowered gloves as though she has worn out her hands on Rupert's body (just as if she had been doing continual washing up) and must at all costs rest and protect them. They say that the morning she has herself carried onto the beach we shall know that Rupert *is* impotent.

8

'The bells are marvellous, Beetle, they clang and clank and hammer themselves to death. Above all they're not tuneful. It's almost as good as St Mark's piazza in Venice; the bells do the same sort of work; a thrilling, transparent evening – just like this one – settles over the buildings. And every now and then a flock of pigeons takes off! It makes you feel you're flying up into the air yourself.'

'Darling, you'd fly beautifully in that yellow velvet cosmonaut suit.' Beetle has put his hand under my arm, he's at least an inch taller than normal (he has a really good sense of occasion in such matters) and his Mr Fish shirt-cuffs, well out over his wrists and fastened with agate knobs (very small, but enough), give his hands a tender, corrupt delicacy. I quickly go over the palm of one of his hands to see whether any luxury bumps have sprung up, which I shall have to cope with. But no, it's just as before, firm and curiously flat. The palm of an intellectual for whom luxury is always an idea imperfectly in focus, not a necessity.

In places the crowd in the piazza is very thick. Certain streetcorners are favoured, the people who mill around there look rich, handsome and lucky. Then suddenly you get a bald patch of ground, which people seem to avoid. Those who take up a position there have a vague feeling that something is wrong; they shift their feet as though they're standing on a grave and know they shouldn't, or have agoraphobia. We keep getting separated.

'Beetle, these coloured lights in great arches are works of art! And look at the bandstand ones! Hullo, are they going to sing?'

'Yes, there's the local bandmaster. God, look at the trombones. They must have been up all night polishing them.'

'With Duro-glit. Shall we go into the church, just to see what's going on? Better hurry, we don't want to miss the procession.'

Everyone moves slowly but with a bustling intensity. Chains of four or five Livonians stroll forward together, a family, linked by their arms. One end of the chain may be very small and sailing a balloon filled with gas; hypnotised by the tugging of the string in its fingers, it is connected to Heaven and you can read the deepest peace in its eyes. At the other end, here is Mammon, the father, with a bronze head and gold teeth; his happiness consists in assuring himself of his temporal identity by greeting as many people as possible with every step.

'Darling, can I buy a chicken-noise?'

The band has struck up *Traviata* – the music comes out in separate lumps like water from a tap with an air-lock in it.

'What?' shouts Beetle.

'One of those little cardboard drums with a string and a piece of resin. You make chicken-noises with it.'

Some local boys pass us making the most excruciating chicken-noises right into our ears. It's highly satisfactory. Beetle at once buys me one for a hundred lire. At the *festa* everything is a hundred lire: the Japanese plastic serpents with red forked tongues and the blocks of nougat the size of a boot and looking like a piece of the living-room wall. We have glimpses of one another when the crowd opens and shuts. We are always in the act of doing impossible things. I know that Dyson and Rety saw us getting a chicken-noise, but then I saw them playing with a tin aeroplane which made sparks in its tail when you ran it along the ground, and which they had no intention of buying.

'There's Rupert with Maddy – dressed from head to toe in white! Gosh, are they already wandering in the Gardens of Marriage?'

'Better keep off gardens,' says Beetle.

'Tennis courts of marriage. I'll ask Maddy how many sets she's played today. The children are still dead keen to weigh her.'

'There they are, with Dirty and Filthy.'

'Ossie says Dirty calls us "flip".'

'I should hate to think what that means.'

'I say, Beetle, do look. James has got Maddy to that weighing machine!'

'Bet you she doesn't get on it.'

'She's looking at the dial. So's Rupert. He's put some money in. Oh, she's put her pekinese on it!'

'That's what they're for.'

'It was a near thing. Suppose it clicked up ten stone with Maddy on it. Rupert could never call her "baby" again.'

We're in the church at last. It's busy, but not too busy,

like Marks and Spencers on an ordinary day. The altar is blazing with very hot flaming candles, some are as thick and white as a human arm. (When Beetle first arrived and went swimming, his arms were no darker, and the sea made fine Italian marble with the flesh on his temples, shoulders, and thighs.) In the chairs and pews, spiritual and secular business is going on. I've just seen one man have a telegram delivered to him where he sits. He made his chair-leg squeak in his enthusiasm. The whispering, pointing, rustling, curtsying to the altar, and the making of the sign of the cross, all provide a focal point of holiness around the wooden figure of the Saint Assunta, patroness of the island. The old are praying; they enjoy having a noise to pray against. There's a rumbling sound from outside. Thunder. The praying rises a semi-tone. Beetle says:

'Darling, you're not going to make a chicken-noise in here, are you?'

'No. I say, there's going to be a storm.'

'That's Purzelbaum clearing his throat. It'll spoil the fireworks.'

'Beetle, just smell the church smell! Incense, damp and marble – it's rather like cold marzipan smell under the icing on a birthday cake. Or like a potato. Carbohydrate, bitter, and refreshing.'

'You need the rumble of thunder to bring it out.'

We buy and light a candle for my mother, and leave through the huge wooden doors.

'Careful. We're part of the procession.'

'I want to hold a candle in a purple plastic flower like these little boys.'

'You can't.'

'I love the priests. That really is dressing up, having two boys to hold your train. Maddy ought to see them.'

'She's just left in a taxi with Rupert. I think it was the thunder.'

'Beetle, you're in among the band, you know.' Beetle jumps as they strike up around him.

Assunta is brought out of the church on a litter at shoulder height. There are canopies carried on poles with tassels which jog to and fro. Bang! The first firework of the evening goes off, splitting the eardrums. No one moves a muscle; you've never seen Italians so expressionless. The procession chants and intones to itself like a dreaming body. Black shoes shuffle about under the heavy gowns. The church rings its bells as though the Devil had hold of the bell-ropes. On top of all this, explosions, thunder, bells and band, there's a deafening mega-blast from the sea. It's the klaxon of the boat which is to take the saint on a short excursion. The boom of it, a whole funnel's worth, is enough to knock your hat off. A good thing Prostitutess left early.

What's this enormous object nosing its way across the path of the procession? A white Rolls-Royce!

'Look who's inside!'

'Who?'

'Chamoun and Killi and Caroline!'

'O God, Beetle, Caroline looks as though she's bricked-in. How lousy for her.'

'She likes it. She's sorry for us not being in one ourselves.'

'Oh no. Caroline's got her poor little white turnip of a face on. That's her bricked-in face.'

'She's as brown as a berry!'

'She's not underneath.'

'The main thing is Killi's caught Chamoun.'

'No, darling, Chamoun's caught Killi. It must be his Rolls. Gosh. I don't know if I'm at a wedding or a funeral.'

'A love affair,' says Beetle; 'just look at their faces! It's like a travelling theatre.'

'They've got their noses together.'

'They'll soon be rubbing them against each other.'

'Are they absolutely ruthless?'

'Oh absolutely.'

'What a relief, Beetle. If people are ruthless you don't have to have a conscience about them.'

As the car can only move very, very slowly, Chamoun and Killi occasionally break off their conversation to look out into the brightly lighted darkness. I can distinctly see Killi taking out a little bottle, unscrewing the cap, and offering something to Chamoun. Sleeping tablets. Killi takes oblong blue capsules with numbers on them which come off on the inside of his stomach. So it's true love! You only give your sleeping tablets up to the partner of your choice. Even so, I ask:

'What's he giving him?'

'Nun's contraceptives. "Wear this for My sake".'

'They keep touching each other.'

'It's called "keeping in touch".'

'Beetle, do you think Killi will manage to put Chamoun in the wrong as he does Caroline?'

'There'll be a terrific struggle in which each tries to put the other in the wrong. Then they'll rest. And start all over again.'

'Who will win?'

'Chamoun. He's got the Rolls.'

'I'm not so sure. Caroline says Killi says you've got to whack them over the head with a penis.'

'A Rolls *is* a penis.'

'Poor Carol. Why should she sit in on their act? They're supposed to be in love with *her*. She looks lost.'

'She'd rather be lost in a Rolls than out of it.'

'Do look. Every now and then they stop whistling at one another and look quickly at Carol. They're afraid she might say something amusing, have an opinion, or even correct a word they mispronounce. And they want to prove to one another that they appreciate sophisticated women, and can break off in the middle of complex discussions and throw them a handful of words to occupy them for the next ten minutes.'

'Lovers are very single-minded.'

'No wonder she's growing a moustache.'

'Chamoun's mixing her a cocktail from that cabinet. She'll like that.'

'If they wore their aprons and Caroline grew her moustache, it would be a draw. She doesn't care tuppence for his phoney cocktail.'

'Oh. Killi's got my Italian phrase-book!'

'Darling, how serious. Shall we rap on the window and ask for it back?'

'He's reading bits out – and Chamoun is going over his hair with a ready hand. Must be the barber's shop dialogue.'

'They're borrowing our fun!'

'They need it in there.'

There's another gigantic clap of thunder and the Rolls moves out of sight back into the crowd. I sniff the air again.

'Thunder is very potatoey.'

'We'll go and eat. Dyson and Rety want us to join them at that restaurant on poles over the water.'

'Why don't they go off and chase women?'

'They're frightened. They're on their own here and out of their depth. They might have to marry someone. It's not like Fleet Street or TV centre, with lots of matching rabbits in rabbit warrens.' (Or, as Dyson said yesterday, 'Well, you don't go to a woman for conversation, do you? Kahk.' No wonder they *rush* him back in London.)

That must be the reason. The girls here are far more beautiful, better dressed, just as clever, and speak English. But they don't know the sick city code, don't live indoors, don't talk about hangovers and parties, aren't accessible morning, noon and night, don't know how to make a telephone lethal or voluptuous. They're healthy (no grey skin) and seem to have time to do what they want; that's enough to put anyone off.

Rety and Dyson have a corner table under an awning. In the water below there are paper cups floating; each contains a lighted candle. The thunder has given the sea some movement, but its black glass is unbroken. Fireworks fall into it every few seconds, we see them coming down in flashes between the awning and the platform. The banging and the smell of saltpetre has invigorated Rety, who is flushed and leaning on a great pile of folded English newspapers which he has just bought. He signals to us as though laying bets:

'I say! I say! Have you seen Purzelbaum?'

'No. Have you?'

'No. And we've looked everywhere ... down among the stalls of clothes and coffee-pots, past those great cement-mixers with hot chocolate beans in them ... not a sign of him. We knew what he'd be wearing. A navy-blue, pin-striped, middle-European suit, very tightly fitting, especially where the coat goes over the behind. Oh dear me, yes. Can't have any sagging or bagging *there*.'

'We were all ready to greet him –'

'Ronald was to sneeze violently, giving him the effect of being on the deck of a ship, and I was to tell him that no English breakfast menu was complete without sausage-meat pie ... gives you hot armpits.'

'Then I was to quote –'

'Ronald was to start off: "Thou still unravished bride of quietness!"'

'To prove I had to leave England because I exulted in my body.'

'When I think of what we nearly missed!' says Beetle.

I have to sit carefully on account of my plunge neckline. As I settle on the chair, I suddenly hear Prostitutess in my head: 'You must *never* wear a long V-neck, darling, because it diminishes the bosom.' To this I remember I answered, 'Isn't that a good thing, if it's a big bosom?' And Prostitutess thundered in reply, 'No bosom, my darling, is ever big enough.'

Damn. I've diminished my bosom on the very evening when I need it. I take a deep breath and put my shoulders back.

Dyson's eyeballs are bloodshot. It's obvious these two

have been drinking themselves into a sullen frenzy over Purzelbaum. But it's so amusing. We must cram them with *Zuppa di pesce* and get them sane again. The atmosphere of the *festa* has got into them; they glance boldly at women sitting at tables near us and lick their lips (once we've given them the safety of our companionship). Their manners are atrocious. Some people never get used to being out of their own country. I'm accustomed to the staccato crackle of Dyson trying to give an order to a waiter – in a country where all the important orders are given in a silky whisper or by narrowing the eyelids – but when he rides on the two back legs of his chair with a large coloured napkin tucked into his collar and says, 'You've got to hand it to the Wops,' I can't help taking back his O level for gardening. As for Rety, his practical joking is quite obviously going to ruin his life. He's just risen up from the table unsteadily and called for a telephone by bellowing:

'Ho there!'

There's a moment's silence from the entire restaurant, so much so that I can distinctly hear the first drops of rain striking the tarpaulin over our heads. English sounds. How cold!

The talk starts again, but everyone has an eye on our table since we're obviously going to provide the real entertainment of the evening.

Rety bends over me and, staring down my V-neck, says:

'I shall say to Purzelbaum, "Now I want you to think very carefully before answering this ..."' He giggles infectiously.

(No bosom, my darling, says Prostitutess, is ever ...)

'David, do sit down, says Beetle, 'you're disorderly.'

'Those are noble breasts!' says Rety *very* unexpectedly.

'You're drunk.' Beetle is sharp. 'Sit down.'

'Mimi,' says Rety, 'for you I prescribe double insomnia tablets, taken three times nightly . . . in case we drop off to sleep . . . And they can carry the flower-heads away afterwards.'

'*David.*'

'Don't be stingy!' says Rety. 'It's supposed to be a holiday. You don't know how boring it is up at Rupert's.'

'You must make your own amusements.'

'I *am*. She's growing those for me.'

There are three things I can do to cure the situation. Make an excruciating chicken-noise, which *could* have the effect of pepping him up. Say that there are mosquitoes under the table, and ask if everyone else is being bitten too. The mere thought that they're being bitten puts men in a frenzy and usually eradicates all other thoughts for up to five minutes. Or, three, take off Rety's mannered drunkenness to his face. I decide on a version of the last one, and say:

'You forgot to go "Hic!"'

A bullseye! Rety stops looking at my V-neck and looks at me, the wind out of his sails. He knows he's been done down, and after staring a bit he manages to think of something.

'Ah!' he gasps to me, 'you have put the brush into my mouth!'

He looks idiotically pleased with himself, and he reaches out for his glass of wine, beginning to intone as he does, 'Bring me my bow of burning gold, and bring me my arrows of diszier . . .' But the low notes defeat him, and his throat rumbles hollowly, so that he has to try all over again: 'Zi-er . . .'

In response the waiter places a huge bowl of steaming *zuppa di pesce* on the table. Blue mussel shells stick out of the sauce of hot oil, wines, and blood-red tomato. It's irresistible.

Rety touches the waiter on the arm and asks with exquisite politeness:

'Will you have the goodness to tell me where is a telephone?'

'Si, signor.'

The waiter guides him across the room and out of sight. Rain hits more noisily overhead. We help ourselves – in fact, I am helped by Beetle – to this red sea food that makes hot water in my mouth as I look at it. Only half an hour ago I was a yellow velvet cosmonaut, aloof, scented, anti-social, all ready to land on the moon or engage in other objective pursuits. Now I am a thing of the earth, my appetite is the size of a boarding school, and if you could see the zestful fashion I get my spoon down along the mother of pearl to where the mussel cushion lies, and dig it off its fixative, you might find it necessary to re-think my character. Yes, you could pass me on Waterloo Station in this mood and say to yourself, 'A genuine proletarian. A straightforward fishwife, with brain, genitals and nerves buried in homely worker's blubber.' At the word 'blubber' I take a much closer look at what I'm eating, now that the edge is off my appetite. There are some very strange objects in this soup – teeth, legs, tentacles. I half expect to find Killi's flipper – the one he lost when Chamoun was pursuing him.

'What have you found?' asks Beetle. 'Byron's slippers?'

Dyson cackles snobbishly.

'They're somewhere around the Mediterranean. And I'm sure they'd make excellent soup,' says Beetle.

'Actually, now you come to mention it!' I stir my remains. 'It's more like a toe.'

Dyson stops eating abruptly.

I suddenly see a way of getting rid of him. There's nothing I want more at the moment than to be alone with Beetle. And Dyson has been lapping at his soup like a ninety-two-year-old bloodhound. If *he's* squeamish how does he think I feel! One of the big brown no-name island dogs is standing by my chair, persistently begging. Now there's nothing more repulsive than a big dog making wolfing, bolting noises, especially when you're gourmand-ising on something that is mid-way between a delicacy and a wholly unmentionable item in the egg or eye category. With my coloured napkin I pick out a morsel and offer it to the dog, which promptly clamps its jaws over it and makes perfect wolfing, bolting noises. Dyson puts his spoon down and breaks bread.

'What was that?' he asks, quaking.

'I think it was what they call a sea-cow or poultice slug. It's a little bit slimy.'

While Dyson is looking faint, I fill in time by charming the dog.

'You can see it's a young one because it hasn't got any wrinkles on its forehead. Poor flea factory!' (That ought to help.)

'I hope that dog knows you're using it as a napkin,' says Beetle, 'under the pretext of stroking it.'

He has my foot gripped firmly between his under the table; Dyson is very definitely *de trop*.

'Go to Ronald for your next sea-slug, dog.' I talk calmly to the dog, showing it the way. It stands by Ronald and dabs some froth on his hand. Then it spreads its great hot jaws along his squeamish thighs and, with both eyes wide open above them, stares up at him placidly. His unhappiness is very great.

'Are you all right, Ronald? It's not . . .' (try to keep the hope out of your voice) 'Livone tummy, is it?'

'Yes, I think it is.'

'Bad luck. Because I know how ghastly it can be. Have you any Entero-vioform, the traveller's friend?'

'No. I don't think so.'

'Oh gosh, Beetle. He hasn't got Entero-vioform.'

'Oh dear. How do you feel?'

'It's a sort of nausea, and . . .'

'Oh dear.'

'I think I may have to go home . . .'

'There's Entero-vioform at the house.'

There's another roar from the thunder, which has been moving up on us all this time, and now seems to be almost directly overhead. I can see Rety returning from his mission with the glass of wine still in his hand. He approaches between the tables, giving out good-humoured glances.

'You can congratulate me,' he says, arriving at our table and thumping himself down.

'David, what have you been up to?'

'I've been doing what I said I would do. Phoning up the good Doctor.'

'Oh God. What did you say?' I can see Rupert going down forever in the middle of a forest of garages.

'I didn't actually *say* anything.'

'You mean he did the talking?'

'Well, no. Actually he didn't really say anything either.'

'Well, somebody must have said something!'

'Not really. You see, I dialled the number, and when he answered, I . . . growled.'

'You *growled*?'

'It was a cross between a growl and a gargle. More of a wowel.'

'What on earth did you do that for?'

'Just' – he smiles with great joy – 'a moment of inspiration.'

'What about Purzelbaum? He must have answered the phone in a way that showed whether or not he had a sexual problem?'

'He just took it off the hook and listened. So I growled.'

There's a further burst of thunder, and all the lights go out. At the first second of darkness, Beetle takes hold of my hand. We're united, and silently bless the weather.

Rety goes on chatting to the darkness; he's fulfilled. The *nicht küssen*, the bathing trunks ignominy, all has been sponged out.

'Mind you, you might say that by the very act of *not* answering the phone, he revealed a hellish libido,' says the darkness.

'That's arrogance, pure and simple,' I reply to it. 'The most an arrogant man will ever say on picking up a phone is "Yes?"'

The lights flash on again, and Dyson is suddenly

revealed as having got rid of the brown no-name dog in some spectacularly abrupt fashion. He composes himself and tries to appear unflurried. Still, he is a very nasty pale green colour. He smiles at us in a sickly way. *Noli-me-dogere*, never.

'I think perhaps I'd better go home.'

'OK. Lost your dog?'

'Yes. He took himself off.'

'Probably heard David growling to himself in the phone-booth.'

'Oh no!' says Rety proudly. 'It was a work of telephone art. Only for His ears. Then I hung up. Ting!'

9

'Of course I was *furious*, darling. It was outrageous. Even now, I can tell you that I am not calm.' All the same, I notice Prostitutess smiles to herself. 'But the Doctor came to me privately and apologised afterwards. And he went to Rupert privately and humbled himself and was very charming.'

Caroline and I are transfixed. We can't take our eyes off her. Even here in the privacy of her bedroom, it may not be quite private enough for her to tell us the full story. We tend to whisper so as to reassure her.

Quite unnecessary. Nothing could stop Prostitutess telling it. If there was a steam-roller clanking past outside, she would tell it. If she was gagged, she would nibble her way through the gag to tell it. She strokes her pekinese and waits modestly to have it dragged out of her. I don't want to make my questions too clinically accurate, and while I'm groping, Caroline, with all her married strength, is able to say:

'But, Maddy, were you and Rupert actually . . . in bed?'

'Too hot, my darling, in that sticky, thundery air; my Rupert hates constricting sheets and clothes. He was stretched out on the bed, without a stitch on, looking *marvellous.* You know his torso is like a man of twenty, so much hard, rich flesh. It takes years to build up the flesh on a body until it is just right. I can tell you between ourselves, he is *in the prime.*'

She looks at us with a jolly smile, as though she's just got a bargain in the sales. How saucy she is!

'His only trouble,' she goes on, 'has been a little bit of neurosis over that nasty garage. Such a vulgar thing to do. And my Rupert is *molto gentile* himself and wouldn't hurt a fly, so he suffers.' She smiles inwardly again at her secrets, you can only see the shadow inside out on her mouth. 'So I have to stroke him, to take his mind off it and relax him. I am very professional of course, beginning at the brow like this . . .'

She puts her two thumbs on the head of her pekinese, and to its surprise makes a number of brisk, sexy movements.

'Gosh,' I say. 'Is that relaxing?'

'Darling, it is *fantastic.* No man can resist it. Even the very difficult knotted-up men will come and whine and beg you to do it to them.'

I can't help laughing to myself at the thought of what Killi will have to go through in bed tonight! Prostitutess says:

'And then you go on down the body, and you mustn't miss an *inch*, because the body feels it, that little inch feels left out. And you don't talk because that interrupts it. And you must remember that the movements are firm. It's not like an English stroking.'

'What is an English stroking like?' asks Caroline, looking back over the lost years.

'Very insipid, darling. It has no authority. It is like smoothing a bedcover on a bed. A big man gets very jumpy if you do that to him.'

'I thought they only got jumpy if you stroked their balls.' Caroline *is* daring.

Prostitutes looks at her attentively; hmm. She decides to release more information.

'It is all right, darling,' she says in the old super-low voice, 'if you stroke them *upwards*. It is only *downwards* that makes them jumpy.'

'Fancy that,' I say, really impressed. 'Glad to get the weight of gravity off them, I suppose.'

'Very glad indeed,' says Prostitutess, massaging her peke upwards to its extreme astonishment.

'So there you were,' Caroline picks up the story, 'half way down Rupert's body, curing his garage neurosis.'

'Yes. He was . . . very, very relaxed. You know, darling, thunder is a very funny thing because it is a good time to make love when it is thundering.'

'And you were . . . just about to?'

'Well . . . yes. You know, the lights keep fusing when there is a thunderstorm on the island. And I was too busy to get up and get a candle.'

'Naturally.'

'And my Rupert did not want me to go away for *one minute*, he is so demanding, thank goodness. And you know, in the darkness, I couldn't hear anything except the thunder and the ticking of his wrist-watch when I was bending down close to him . . .'

'And?'

'And then, my darling, it was outrageous! It was the

most disgraceful thing! Because the lights went on suddenly – we had forgotten all about them!'

'Of course.'

'Yes, they went on, and, you know, for a moment you are blinded when that happens.'

'Definitely.'

'I was just looking up, and blinking my eyes, and there was the Doctor in the doorway!' She gives a little shrill scream as if he's there again now.

'*No!*'

'Yes, my darling! As large as life, and with my Rupert lying there *in flagrante*!'

It's Lytton and Carrington all over again!

The pekinese jumps off her lap with a sharp bark, looking badly mauled.

'You know something?' Prostitutess says reminiscently.

'No, what?'

'I don't think I would have seen him if he hadn't turned up the little microphone of his hearing aid, because it makes a pent-up shriek, like the top-knot on a pressure cooker when you've got too much inside it.'

'Afraid of missing something, I suppose,' says Caroline rather unnecessarily.

'Well, there you are,' says Prostitutess. 'I just took one look at him! I could have turned him to stone!'

'What did he do?'

'He left *at once*, of course. One minute he was there, and the next he was gone. It was all over in an instant. Bing-bang. Like that.' She looks pleased with herself.

'I should think so. God, what a night!'

'You're telling me, darling. You can imagine my feelings.

I was simply *bouleversé*. Outraged! But at the same time ... after all ... you can understand that in *one* way I couldn't help feeling that my Rupert was ... cleared. Because you have heard that ridiculous story, that rumour, so private and intimate that I'm surprised the Doctor had the shame to associate himself with it?' She's blushing and bridling up, and asks us with flushed cheeks.

'Oh well ...' says Caroline.

'Ah! So you see, you had heard it. What an unscrupulous action that was. But still, the truth is stronger. And now the truth is out.'

'And we'll spread it abroad,' says Caroline. 'But so discreetly, Maddy, that people will just catch on without having to be told anything in so many words. They'll take it in through their pores.'

Prostitutess looks down, as meek and pretty a leg of mutton as you could see anywhere. I get up and kiss her warmly. Being near her is simply delicious, so sweet-smelling, reassuring and gentle is her form.

Caroline asks in a puzzled voice:

'But, Maddy, what made Purzelbaum come over? Was he just nosey-parkering?'

'Well, no. You see, I must admit to you, it was the goodness of his heart. His great heart as a diagnostician. Because he thought that Rupert was very ill. He was afraid that he was dying.'

'But why on earth should he suddenly get the idea that Rupert was dying?'

'Because his telephone rang, and when he picked it up he couldn't hear anything at first. So he turned his deaf aid right up, and then it was very loud and nearly deafened him!'

(We can't help laughing a bit at this sally.)

'What did it say?'

'The Doctor says it made a curious noise, but he has heard it before many times in his long career in medicine. It is the sound a man makes, my darling, when he is trying to speak but he cannot because maybe he has a sudden paralysis, a stroke or something, and he cannot form the words. It is very sad. And when he heard it, the Doctor naturally recognised it at once. And he went to get his bag with an injection for heart attack, and came straight over to Rupert's.'

'How did he know it was Rupert?'

'He guessed. You know, he has this second sight. And there are not many private telephones on the island. Rupert is his oldest friend, so naturally he came to him first, in case it was him.'

'But it *wasn't* Rupert.'

'No. It was not. But it was the right thing to do, so I cannot really be angry with him. And you see, he came to the house, and then suddenly bang! All the lights went off. And the poor Doctor was groping his way along in the dark, and listening for some more of the sounds . . . like the sounds on the telephone . . . in case my poor Rupert had fallen down somewhere and was lying there . . .'

'And all the time you were stroking each other, and not making a sound!'

'Well, I would not say that we were dumb absolutely.' (Tell the truth, Maddy!) 'But we were very, very quiet.'

'With just Rupert's watch ticking? As in a Rolls Royce?'

'Yes . . . And, you see, he could not find Rupert, and he was listening and groping . . .'

'Hist! What's that?' says Caroline gruffly in her imitation of Purzelbaum.

'Until the lights went on!'

'Found him all right then!' says Caroline, laughing rather more boisterously than I would have expected.

'Yes, he was simply astonished. I have never seen a man look so flabbergasted.'

'Bowled over. Couldn't believe his eyes.'

'I think it made him re-adjust his ideas. And now we can be friends again, because it was a generous act to come to rescue Rupert like that, and they are talking to one another just as before.'

Prostitutess laces her fingers after having accomplished this happy ending. *He can, and I've proved it. Amen.*

As for me, *as for me,* I'm back in last night's restaurant looking at David Rety's face. Guilt! Practical-joking journalist, you nearly went too far that time! But what an excellent story. I had no idea human life was going to be so interesting. Oh, I can't wait with my story and my laughter, to take it all to Beetle. Beetle, with whom I made love for three hours last night – no wonder I'm in such high spirits! Afterwards we kept blowing our noses, because sex makes snot. And today I'm so adjusted and integrated with society, I'm simply impossible and don't know what to do with my good fortune and gaiety.

Just as we're going, Prostitutess says mischievously:

'So you know now, darlings, that all the real sex, the real love begins at forty. You don't suppose that phrase "Life begins at forty" is an empty one, do you?' She is sizzling with triumph. 'Unfortunately you have to spend all the years until then learning how to live. That is the boring part. Waterloo will tell you. The first half of life is when you are educating yourself for the good time in the second half. I know my Jung.' (!) 'I feel so sorry for all the young people crawling around on the floor, having emotions. They are so busy being young they haven't time for anything else. Why, you can't even get *real* sex except after a long relationship, two or three years at the very least.'

'It doesn't peter out?'

'It grows as big as a quadruple bed! Yes, after thirty-two, when we have the wife's first flight from the too-small marriage bed – because she wants some *sleep*, darling – after that, it is all much better organised, and quite shameless. As for the change of life, I never felt better! But do keep off the sleeping tablets – *les pilules,* the curse of modern society.'

Ah Prostitutess, how shall we manage on our own without you? I feel as helpless as a tadpole.

The sunshine is especially brilliant outside after a conversation with Prostitutess and after the great wash the sky had in the night. Caroline and I stroll together, looking into shops. Everything sparkles. Presently we dare to look at one another, as if we've been let out of school and have just been given our blue Equity cards so that we can play full-blooded parts in life. Caroline says:

'Hum. It's all very well. But Maddy doesn't know everything. For example, with Killi sometimes the strain between us is so awful, we both start giggling and make friends in the middle!' She starts her chuckle. 'The strain, the pressure, the screaming tension, ha-ha-ha.'

'You're very cheerful today.'

'*My* businessman doesn't need massage.'

'Oh, so that's it! That was powerful thunder last night.'

'Fabulous! Shall we go and sit at a café in the piazza for ten minutes? We shan't have many more times.'

'Don't. I can't bear to go. No more blue Italian money with Verdi on it.'

'No more impossible Viennese doctors – Oh look, there he is!'

Yes, there he is, out in the open, like a great spider folded down to normal size to fit into a cane chair. He's sitting there with his legs wide apart, I'm happy to see, and deep in conversation – with Dyson, of all people. Oh, Livone tummy, that's it. Dyson has befriended him. We sit a few tables away, careful not to interrupt, and are at once totally silent, straining our ears.

'. . . and tell me, Doctor, when I talk to you like this, man to man, as we are now' (the Doctor is wildly alert) 'can you comprehend what I say to you?' Dyson is playing up to him like a brainy little fox-terrier with its favourite man.

'Why, yes,' Purzelbaum answers, bewildered.

'I'm so glad.' Dyson's TV warmth is as good as a five-bar electric fire. Purzelbaum warms himself, almost spreading his hands. 'I'm so glad because it was the same with my grandmother.' (?) 'She was also as deaf as a stone, but if I spoke to her patiently as I am speaking to you now . . .'

Good old Dyson. For one awful moment I thought he was going to change.

I leave you to imagine Purzelbaum's face as Dyson goes on describing his deafness to him. Two little pouches of venom appear slowly at the corners of his mouth. Mind your pouches, Sonny Jim.

Caroline says in a low voice:

'He made the same face when he saw Ossie carrying the tortoises after Dyson "did" his garden. As if they'd gnawed his garden roots. And he'd like to hire them to gnaw off a piece of Rupert's anatomy in return!'

'Now, Carol. We simply must calm down for London.'

'Yes, of course we must.' Caroline's face becomes proper.

'We can't go back like this, jolly and sexed-up; we'll lose all our friends.'

'We're sure to have a terrible journey. That'll get us back to normal.'

'Rupert's given me a dirty pot he dug up, so we've got something to show for the holiday. I think the Greeks must have thrown it out.'

'Just what we need. When you think about it, there really wouldn't have been a holiday but for Rupert . . . and Maddy.'

'And Purzelbaum's behaviour. You know why he behaves like that, don't you? Waterloo explained it to me. It's because he's a refugee, and therefore he has a basic emotional insecurity. It upsets people's moral values when they've suffered a great deal, and if they do outrageous things it's because they are always mentally guests in other people's countries, and find it difficult to be balanced and non-malicious.'

'Poor darling. With his baths. It's very touching.'

I hum, and then put words to it:

' "Out in the open with everyone looking
And everyone laughing and saying What-ho!

She took her bath in the open – to paint it.
And what's wrong with that?
That's what I'd like to know."

'Beetle taught me that. By the way, where are they?'

'Killi and Beetle and Chamoun have gone off together. I rather get the impression – you know Killi won't say anything definite – they're going to bring the garage down about one and a half foot. I think Killi's hired some men, and it's all to be done like lightning, before Purzelbaum goes home. It'll make all the difference to Rupert. And everyone hopes that Purzelbaum won't actually register the new height, just think there's something wrong with himself. After all, the garage will still be there.'

'Killi gets things done. He's absolutely splendid.'

'Isn't he!'

'You know, Carol –'

'I know.'

I can see from Carol's eyes that Killi is her baby again. 'When he is good, he's very, very good, and when he's bad, he's horrid.'

'You looked awfully miserable in the Rolls.'

'That was only because I wasn't driving.' A good and loyal answer.

'What was the cocktail like?'

'Rotten. But it made them happy. So I put up with it.'

'They were killing.'

'I know. They both got drunk before they'd even taken a sip.'

'Just shows you what atmosphere can do. Do you know when I woke up this morning I realised I was *still drunk*?'

'Are you going to marry Beetle?'

'I'm so in love with him, I just can't think clearly. He's the light of my life. But is marriage a good thing?'

'On the whole, not bad at all.'

'Then I think I will. If he still wants to.'

All the suitcases are out. Each of us is trying to dry a wet, salt bathing towel. Or doing long division sums on our beds to see how much money we've got. The sheer arithmetic you have to do on a holiday is appalling, not to mention parking tortoises etc. Am I brown enough to go back? I look at my arms, and then use a hand-mirror. A great improvement. If you work too hard with your brain in London, your features get lumpy and slip out of position. When I've got brain fag, my nose sheers off to the left. And I've noticed that when Beetle has had a tough day his left eyebrow gets fixed up in the air and won't come down for hours.

People keep sneaking off to say goodbye to Purzelbaum; it's amazing. Now Beetle's done it. I'll have to go next, but I'm scared to death of the folds of that white medical kaftan of his, that muddy tent which could wrap itself around me. And I don't want my fingers pinched just before a long journey. Still, I'll have to go. I know; I'll wear gloves and carry one of the tortoises. He can pinch that.

The children spent the morning getting Chamoun's Rolls on board the car ferry. The chauffeur was very patient. It's gone now, carried over a transparent, lulling sea to Pozzuoli, with its cocktail cabinet and its clock ticking away like Rupert in the dark.

Yes, I'm voluptuously tired, just as I ought to be. You really need a holiday to get over a holiday. All the same, I'm ready for the next new bit of life – with Beetle, my one and only Beetle. I'd no idea happiness was so pleasant. I've always lived as if it was more or less irrelevant.

The children are mending our travelling torch in the sitting-room. It's an English one, and you have to doctor it all the time.

James says:

'You've got to stretch the spring. It's not pushing the battery up.'

Tim says firmly:

'No. It's because when you put the bottom on, it won't wind up properly on the worm.'

Ossie says:

'It's the bulb. It's not touching that metal piece underneath.'

'It works if you press the button slightly to the side and hold it.'

'You've only got to put some paper in to lift the battery up.'

'If you screw the bulb right down, it'll work.'

Nearly there already.

VINTAGE CLASSICS

Vintage launched in the United Kingdom in 1990, and was originally the paperback home for the Random House Group's literary authors. Now, Vintage comprises some of London's oldest and most prestigious literary houses, including Chatto & Windus (1855), Hogarth (1917), Jonathan Cape (1921) and Secker & Warburg (1935), alongside the newer or relaunched hardback and paperback imprints: The Bodley Head, Harvill Secker, Yellow Jersey, Square Peg, Vintage Paperbacks and Vintage Classics.

From Angela Carter, Graham Greene and Aldous Huxley to Toni Morrison, Haruki Murakami and Virginia Woolf, Vintage Classics is renowned for publishing some of the greatest writers and thinkers from around the world and across the ages – all complemented by our beautiful, stylish approach to design. Vintage Classics' authors have won many of the world's most revered literary prizes, including the Nobel, the Booker, the Prix Goncourt and the Pulitzer, and through their writing they continue to capture imaginations, inspire new perspectives and incite curiosity.

In 2007 Vintage Classics introduced its distinctive red spine design, and in 2012 Vintage Children's Classics was launched to include the much-loved authors of our childhood. Random House joined forces with the Penguin Group in 2013 to become Penguin Random House, making it the largest trade publisher in the United Kingdom.

@vintagebooks